YOU KNOW WHERE TO FIND ME
Rachel Cohn

SIMON & SCHUSTER BOOKS FOR YOUNG READERS
New York London Toronto Sydney

SIMON & SCHUSTER BOOKS FOR YOUNG READERS
An imprint of Simon & Schuster Children's Publishing Division
1230 Avenue of the Americas, New York, New York 10020

This book is a work of fiction. Any references to historical events, real people, or real locales are used fictitiously. Other names, characters, places, and incidents are products of the author's imagination, and any resemblance to actual events or locales or persons, living or dead, is entirely coincidental.

SIMON & SCHUSTER BOOKS FOR YOUNG READERS is a trademark of Simon & Schuster, Inc.
Book design by Ann Zeak
The text for this book is set in Bembo.
Manufactured in the United States of America
10 9 8 7 6 5 4 3 2 1
Library of Congress Cataloging-in-Publication Data
Cohn, Rachel.
You know where to find me / Rachel Cohn. — 1st ed.
p. cm.
Summary: In the wake of her cousin's suicide, overweight and intro-verted seventeen-year-old Miles experiences significant changes in her relationships with her mother and father, her best friend Jamal and his family, and her cousin's father, while gaining insights about herself, both positive and negative.
ISBN-13: 978-0-689-87859-6 (hardcover)
ISBN-10: 0-689-87859-1 (hardcover)
[1. Suicide—Fiction. 2. Interpersonal relations—Fiction. 3. Overweight persons—Fiction. 4. Substance abuse—Fiction. 5. Family life—Washington (D.C.)—Fiction. 6. Self-esteem—Fiction. 7. Washington (D.C.)—Fiction.] I. Title.
PZ7.C6665You 2008
[Fic]—dc22
2007000851

For Patty

ACKNOWLEDGMENTS
With love and thanks to Patricia McCormick,
Andi Gitow, Dr. Juhayna Kassem, David Levithan,
Linda Braun, and Alissa Merrill.

"Sybylla, Sybylla," said auntie sadly, as if to herself. "In the first flush of girlhood, and so bitter. Why is this?" "Because I have been cursed with the power of seeing, thinking, and worse than all, feeling, and branded with the stinging affliction of ugliness," I replied.

—FROM *MY BRILLIANT CAREER* BY MILES FRANKLIN

Once Upon a Time

⸙

ONCE UPON A TIME, THERE WAS AN UPTIGHT COLLECTOR man named Jim. In the late middle age of his life, Jim decided he wanted a baby with a passion greater even than the obscure Picasso sketch or rare Russian-dynasty Fabergé egg he coveted at the elite auctions he frequented. Apparently being gay, sterile, and old were not factors that should stop Jim from realizing the baby dream. He was independently wealthy, he could make his own dreams happen. So Jim got his beautiful young lover, a Legolas clone but normal-size and from this dimension, to do his thing into a cup. Jim found the perfect surrogate mother, a fit and attractive, penniless medical student who looked like a poor man's Gwyneth Paltrow. If she could do him this favor, he could put her through medical school.

Once upon a time, Laura was born to this man whose greatest wish was to become a father.

Laura fulfilled Jim's every dream of fatherhood.

Good-natured, bright, and adorable, baby Laura was Jim's sun. The dark side was Jim's lover, who'd been holding back a secret. If he didn't take his meds, bad things happened.

Once upon a time, Jim's lover decided he didn't want to take lithium anymore. Before Laura's first birthday, he was dead. But Jim would survive. He had nothing but time and money—and Laura. Raising her would give his advancing years purpose and inspiration, a renewed heartbeat.

Once upon a time, the dead lover's penniless twin sister Melanie appeared at Jim's house in Georgetown, a baby on her hip. Jim took in Mel and her daughter and gave them the carriage house at the back of his property to live in. Jim liked to save people. It was like a rich man's hobby for him. Mel and Jim could raise their children—who were biological cousins—together, almost like sisters.

Mel's child was me, Miles. People assume I'm named after the jazzman Miles, and I don't bother to correct them. People are like that, judging you before they know you. Let them. In fact, I'm named after the feminist Australian author Miles Franklin, an author whose books I'm sure my mother has never touched, much less read. There was a movie made of this author's most famous book, called *My Brilliant Career*, that Melanie and Buddy, my father, saw on their first date. Mel's interest in the movie and the name Miles turned out to be more permanent than her attachment to Buddy. He was out of the picture by the time we arrived at Jim's, seeking shelter and family, a lifeline.

When Laura and I were old enough to safely climb trees, Jim had a tree house built for us in an ancient oak tree on his property. The house was nestled into a branch so full and solid, it was almost its own tree, and not even the seasonal nor'easters passing through could knock it down. The tree house's small window view swished with green leaves and sucked in the heavy, humid D.C. swamp air, sweetened by the faint honeysuckle scent wafting up from the garden. It was our own little paradise, solid.

In that tree house, Laura directed our play time in her favorite game, Once upon a Time. She started the game in her little-girl whisper, her fairy-blond hair and doll-perfect facial features offset by hard blue eyes and the determined clench of her jaw: *Once upon a time, Sleeping Beauty took a nap.* In Laura's fairy tales games, Cinderella never escaped the scullery to meet her prince, Belle left the Beast for the sorceress who'd cast the original spell on him, and that spaz, Alice in Wonderland, needed special pills to make it through her adventures with the looking glass. Villains made no special guest appearances in our Once upon a Time story games. They scared Laura and bored me, so instead we made up heroines with ghastly itchy skin but magnificent tresses of hair, and the occasional sleeping disorder. Those heroines had enough on their hands without having to worry about warding off true evil.

In Laura's favorite story, Sleeping Beauty never woke

up. This made for a short game, but that was fine. While my Sleeping Beauty—Laura—napped in the tree house, I read books, nestled next to her. On scorching summer days, we'd bring a bucket of ice along with us up to the tree house, and I'd rub Sleeping Beauty's hot arms while burying my face in a book, my secret pleasure. Although I could read by age four, I was actively encouraged *not* to read by the time I was in elementary school. I read too much, to the point of being punished, relegated by many a teacher to the corner of the schoolroom in disgrace, my nose to a white, wordless wall that I imagined covered in newspaper print to pass the time. Bruises mapped my body from bumping into tables and tripping over curbs while walking with a book in my hand, my eyes focused on the pages instead of the live space around me.

I preferred books to people. Laura was my exception. We had our own secret language, nonsense words to communicate when adults were present. *Me-oh-my-oh-milo, eh foo manchu mysteryahoyatolah,* in the car ride back from gymnastics class, could translate as, "Miles, since I'm allowed to check out more than two books a week from the library, I snuck some Nancy Drews and the book with the horrible skin-pigment pictures up into the tree house for you." *Aiieee, hersheyhialeaLauraho spaghetti-o-saurus* was easily understood as "I swiped some chocolate bars for us from 7-Eleven, Laura. Meet you up there after dinner." When we fell over each other in giggles on the backseat of Jim's sedan, we could look up to the rearview mirror to see Jim's sandy-gray eyebrows lifted in amusement, his blue-gray eyes fixed on us, our secrets secure in his ignorance and his joy in us.

Laura and I never went to the same school, but we did everything else together: Brownies and Girl Scouts, summer camp, swimming and dance lessons. With our white-blond hair and rosy complexions, we were often mistaken as sisters. To us, "cousin" meant almost the same thing as "sister"—inseparable, but with separate houses. While Laura's social schedule brimmed with invitations as mine never would, she refused to go to sleepovers or birthday parties without me. When the thunderous storms that rocked the Potomac passed by at night, I slipped across the courtyard to her house, up to her room, where the princess's queen-size bed had plenty of extra space for me. I needed it. On that giant bed, I huddled next to her and made up stories to drown out the crackling sky that cracked open terror in Laura's heart.

Once upon a time, adolescence came along and pulled us apart. Laura grew into the goddess her genetic predetermination had promised. Tall, slim, and still fairy-haired blond, popular, academically gifted, and with the inevitable all-star boyfriend, Laura was the perfect progeny Jim had bet he could create.

Once upon a time, two cousins who loved each other like sisters turned back into cousins, polite and tolerant of one another, disinterested.

Laura's light burned so bright, it blinded me. I slipped into darkness. I live on a diet of Hostess snacks, greasy

Chinese food, Cokes, and smokes. I bury the tonnage packed onto the generous curves of my chest and hips under billowing black dresses, leg fat wrapped into black tights, feet smothered in too-tight black boots. Depending on the day's humidity, my long, thick hair falls somewhere between curly and frizzy—but never lustrous. My hair is dyed black but I'm lazy with the roots, as with everything else, so the artificial black hair peeks natural blond at the top, giving me a bloated, inverted porcupine-color look. Where Laura's face bursts with bright blue eyes, peach cheeks, and pink lips, mine is powdered a death pallor, accentuated by a nose stud and a lip ring, and my baby-blue eyes, the same shape and color as Laura's, are heavily lined with a kohl pencil, my mouth painted in the deep Popsicle-purple of a good bruise.

They call me "8 Mile" at school—white trash with the wide load, capable of an occasional decent rap. I'm the token white girl at a D.C. charter school that's 70 percent black, 20 percent Hispanic, 5 percent Caucasian, 4 percent Asian, and 1 percent fat (me). Teachers say I'm a natural-born writer. What I really am is a natural-born reader. I may write stories during class to pass the time ticking away at my boredom, and I may sometimes let my best friend Jamal turn my words into performance art, but I plan on pledging foremost allegiance to books written by other people. I would have nothing to say if I ever tried to be a real writer. My life is a waste not worth reporting. Whereas, even bad books are rarely boring.

Words jump. Pages fly. Action. 8 Mile observes it all, but does not live it.

Teachers say they can't understand why I turn in work late or not at all, why I don't care if I maintain a C-average. If only I tried, I could be a star student. Trying is overrated. Trying earns teacher comments like "excellent thesis statement, but improper use of commas" (so, what) or "this reads like you wrote it during lunch right before it was due instead of drafting and revising for the last two weeks, per the assignment requirement" (french fry spots on notebook paper, always, give me, away).

When the school term ends, this supposed natural-born writer will be lucky to pass Creative Writing. She is, however, acing gym. Fat girls can kickbox something fierce.

Those teachers won't have to worry about me being a letdown once school lets out. I don't plan on returning to school for senior year. I turn eighteen at the end of August. I don't have to go back if I don't want to. I can do what I want with my life.

I should have graduated with Laura and Jamal this past May. But once upon a time, the most gifted reader in her kindergarten class was held back. The parent/teacher/principal conference in which I had no vote determined that my social skills were not on par with the rest of the erudite Play-Doh set, and I would be better served by repeating kindergarten. So began my life of utter academic boredom. It shall end when school lets out next week. I have the summer to figure out a plan of escape. I cannot do another year of school. I will not. I will pass a million times through Dante's Inferno before walking through the doors of high school again.

I know where I will go to figure out my escape plan, and I know who will help me. The tree house is still a sanctuary, where Laura and I occasionally have our happy medium. She surprised us by breaking up with her boyfriend soon before graduation; we expected her to follow him to Boston in the fall. Blessed with a multitude of thick-enveloped Ivy League acceptances, she chose Georgetown. She is not ready to leave home. I am not ready to let her go.

Laura returned to me this past spring, to our tree house. In the late afternoons after school, when no else is around, we know without communicating, and instinctively she'll show up in the tree house when I've scored a nickel bag, and I can sense when she's up there with a pill. Here, Miles, a 40-gram for you, a 20-gram for me. You crush, together we'll snort. 8 Mile's body weight can sustain the Oxy40, but pixie-perfect Laura can't tolerate past a 20.

Two girls who share nothing now except some genes and a shared childhood still have one thing in common. They like to get high. A joint, sometimes an Oxycontin, usually a Percoset, these are our weapons of choice, missiles that rocket us to a place where we feel nothing except quiet and the wet air, the hum of crickets ushering in dusk, the suspension of anxiety, empty brains beaming laser light shows.

I haven't yet told Laura of my plan to drop out of school because why waste a good high with discussion? I will get around to telling her soon. I will get her to the bookstore alone, and we won't be high, and I will tell her, and she will help me.

Once upon a time, two sister-cousins played together in the musty aisles of the neighborhood bookstore. The fairy-tale stories they acted out there were so entrancing, the owner renamed the store for them. Later he hired the head storyteller. Once upon a Time, the bookstore where I now work part-time (or, basically, whenever I bother to show up), is off the beaten Georgetown path, situated on a garden-filled, brick-lined side street of Federal-era row houses, a hangout for locals, university students, and the occasional lost tourist. Unlike the chain stores in the nearby Wisconsin and M Street corridor, with their generic cafés, immaculate shelves brimming with shiny new books and admirable collections of pretty writing journals, the store where I work is a dusty old place with mildewed walls; it's lined with stacks of old magazines and wobbly bookcases shelving spy mysteries and pulp fiction, new and antiquarian books, in no particular order. There's no saving this place, so we don't bother with a Self-Help section. We do have a cappuccino machine, but it only works if you kick it a certain way, and it's only used in situations of dire caffeine emergency. The store makes no money whatsoever, and I suspect the only reason it stays in business is as a tax write-off for the owner. In truth, the store is a dump. But it's my dump, my second home since childhood, the place I could be found on the days I "forgot" to go to school.

But then.

Once upon a time, a week after Laura's graduation ceremony, Jamal came into the bookstore. He did not offer his usual greeting, "Yo, Miles, turn that frown upside down," spinning the cliché with a stream of back-beats coming from all corners of his mouth. In fact, it was the first time since I've known him that Jamal's mouth was clamped tight, teeth gritted, his dark eyes fogged to a place no blunt could take them. I knew right away, he hadn't dropped by for any of his usual missions. He was not here to enlist me to apply for asylum at the Canadian Embassy, to kidnap me to Adams-Morgan for some jerk chicken and the reggae record store afterward, or to offer me a commission for holding the money can while he breakdanced with his crew, back flips and full-circle head spins from the ground, for tourists down by the C&O Canal.

Jamal is the only reason 8 Mile has survived high school this far. His mom is friends with Laura's dad, so it seems like I've known him my whole life, but it wasn't until we ended up at the same high school that we became friends. Early freshman year, I was carrying my lunch tray to a solitary corner of the cafeteria when I accidentally bumped into one of the school's generic mean girls. "Watch your step, *8 Mile*," Mean Girl snapped at me, in front of a crowded table of popular kids. Before I had a chance to sink inside humiliation, Jamal stood up from that table, took the tray from my hands, and placed it next to his lunch. "I *wish* I could skat like this girl," he said. He placed his arm across my shoulders for all to see. "Y'all heard those Black Panther raps she wrote for the oral project in History of Social Movements class? 'Stoked to be Stokely.' Wish I'd thought of it."

Since that moment, Jamal and I have been like the mismatched pairing in a Hollywood buddy movie, only in our D.C. version, it's Freak Girl befriended by Popular Boy not so they can bring down a drug cartel, etcetera, but maybe because Jamal's simply like that: kind. He's the actor-rapper-breakdancer boy who can do anything, including shroud 8 Mile in secondhand cool, her association with him saving her lily-white ass from being kicked on a regular basis. He's the one person who can coax me out of a book and into the world. Sometimes I think of Jamal as a literary character from an anthology of my favorite books: His charisma is part Salinger's Zooey Glass, coated in the brown sugar of Tea Cake from *Their Eyes Were Watching God*, with the sly cool of a Dashiell Hammett detective, and the hot looks of a Walter Mosley one. He'd be played by a young Mos Def in the movie, sound track by old school Stevie Wonder.

Inside my bookstore, Jamal said only, "Laura . . ." And I knew, just knew by the rip through my gut and the instant convulsion in my heart, knew by Jamal's uncharacteristically unsmiling face. I knew because Laura always did what I wished I could do. My mother must have sent Jamal to deliver the news that, now twice struck, she could not handle a second time.

Characters can shape-shift, switch allegiances, turn back time and come back from the dead, at the writer's direction. I could do none of those things for Laura.

Once upon a time, Sleeping Beauty decided to take a nap from which she would never wake up.

Love Letter to Percoset:
A User Review by Miles

Say you're bored. Or you can't sleep. Maybe your mom is yelling at you, or the boy/girl you like doesn't like you back in that same way, or you're too fat to even consider going to prom. Or the closest person to you since you were babies in the cradle together has killed herself. The usual stuff.

Dread not. Don't be depressed. Be a junkie!

You can't count on people to nurture you through the trauma that is existence. But you already knew that. But did you know that you *can* always count on Percoset?

How-to:

Perc-popping is not a group experience. Dare to fly solo. It's yours to enjoy on your own—

chemical self-pleasure routing that tired old classic, your hand.

Start by drawing the shades in your bedroom. Welcome the darkness. Lift the pill from your nightstand, clutch the water glass in your hand. Offer up your divine thanks in advance. Be greedy—swallow the pill whole rather than split it in half to spread the wealth for a later date. Dilution is wasteful. Savor the wholesome wholeness.

Now lay down in bed. Close your eyes.

Wait.

Just a little longer.

Feelin' it now? The tingle starting at the ends of your toes, creeping inside the tips of your fingernails? Smiiiiiiile. Yeah! The tingle spreads, mushrooming throughout your body, but not in a harsh, Hiroshima way. Only beauty.

Welcome!

You're light as a feather, happy as a lottery winner who doesn't have to pay taxes on their winnings. You are now high, even if in the Perc context that word is a misnomer. (That means a wrong or inappropriate name for all you non-SAT-studying stoners out there.) You're not amphetamine high, bouncing out of your skin with energy, or psychedelic, LSD high. You're velvet high. Completely relaxed. Numb.

Think as if you are in a waking dream. Choose

the fantasy—you direct it, and not it, you. The world is a nice place. Suffering does not exist. Your American president, the supposed leader of the free world, is not in fact ruining the environment, the economy, your future. The boy/girl you love loves you back—he/she might even ask you to prom! The one person on Earth you expected to walk through life with you chose to give you warning that she was shortcutting out, that she no longer wanted to live. She told you good-bye. She at least invited you to come with her.

Mummify yourself inside your bed's blankets—coffinlike, but not dead. Feel your body float away. Bye-bye, body, bye-bye! Heaviness transformed into nothingness.

Magic. You control the knobs.

Let your thoughts run free, as if your mind is taking a leisurely Sunday afternoon walk through a garden in spring bloom. Stop and whisper to the flowers, the violets and marigolds and gardenias, and don't ignore the carnations because they're a cheap variety. All this time, you thought the flowers were just pretty things. Turns out, they've been waiting for you to acknowledge the secret language they'll share only with you, and with puppies. Absorb their flower wisdom. Listen in peace rather than engage.

Aw, puppies. They're never not happy to see you.

Let the pretty pretties, petunias and puppies, lull you to sleep. Sleep sleep sleep, precious one. Sleep until your body is ready to return to the mother ship. Freefalling dreams with safe landings.

Beautiful violet-velvet coma-coffin. Praise be!

Worry not that upon waking, nothing in the world around you will have changed, other than your increasing desire for more Percs.

Was this review helpful to you?
☐ Yes   ☐ No

Braids

LAURA IS DEAD BUT I AM HAVING A GOOD HAIR DAY.

Niecy braids my hair while I eat handfuls of plain M&Ms and we watch cartoons, the deepest form of entertainment we can tolerate today. We've been sitting in the living room of the carriage house for two hours, and the braids are almost finished. I like braids okay. I always like M&Ms. I don't like TV, except for today.

My porcupine hair has been tamed, cornrowed into dozens of braids, with crystal beads, the expensive ones, hanging from the ends. Niecy and I chose the beads in honor of Laura—her eyes, and her spirit, both baby blue. Laura loved my hair done up in braids by Jamal's little sister. Niecy's hands have been extra gentle all morning, pulling the braids tight but sneaking in soft touches on my scalp, reassuring rubs on my shoulders. I don't like to be touched, except for today.

Niecy stands in front of me, ready to braid the last

section of hair at the side of my face. She admires the nearly complete result of her labor. I haven't gotten around to putting on "the darkness," as Jamal calls my cosmetic choices, and with my hair pulled back and no black eyeliner or Goth lipstick coloring my face, it's possible to see I have one. "You have such a pretty face," Niecy says, in her matter-of-fact voice that goes beyond her fifteen years. The remaining, unspoken part of her sentence, of course, is: *for a fat girl*. That's always the implied ending of anyone telling me I have "such a pretty face." "You should show it off more. But I can't believe Jamal let you get a lip ring."

I tell her, "You see, Niecy, I have this extraordinary power. It's called 'free will.' Jamal's girlfriends don't know how to use it when he's telling them what to wear to parties so they'll look good at his side, but unlike those hoochie mamas, I actually have a mind of my own."

She laughs and I laugh, and then at the same time, we look at each other and stop laughing. Today is Laura's funeral and nothing is funny, except maybe the animated figures on the TV, who normally are not funny at all.

Years from now, if I make it that far: How will I remember this day? That I neglected to grieve because I was laughing, having my hair braided, and eating candy but picking out the red M&Ms because they creeped Laura out? Laura hated the color red for no reason other than Because I Just Do. She loved blue and yellow; green didn't offend her although she didn't necessarily like it, but red? Fireworks. She'd burn wrong-colored presents anyone might have innocently given her, a red scarf, a red bracelet. Red books she'd pass off to me. I could read them if I promised to keep them hidden from her sight.

The M&M sugar rush eases my morning-after Perc headache, the price I sometimes pay for beauty's velvet night sleep. Must remember: Bedtime sorrow is for Vicodin (name-brand *or* generic hydros, must not be a snob). The bummer with hydros is, you don't come down slow at all, you just all of a sudden realize it's gone. But while the high isn't as intense, the morning after awakens smoother—pink instead of black.

I am trying not to think of the colors Laura saw at the end, but I can't help it. I am dying to know. I guess I can't use that expression anymore. Can I?

When Laura passed over from darkness into light— or was it the other way around?—I want to know what she saw. Were there people waiting for her, or WELCOME signs, hopefully in blues and yellows? Or was there just nothingness? No color, not even gray? I know there was no God waiting for her, because no God could have let her find Him this soon.

Who will look after Sleeping Beauty on the other side? Who will tell her stories and rub ice on her arms when she's hot? I am scared for her, even as I envy her.

Laura was considerate, as always. And not cheap. She wanted an anonymous person to find her, not me, not Jim. She checked into the deluxe suite at the fanciest five-star hotel in Georgetown. She spent her last afternoon there, with the drapes drawn, lying on the plush bed with headphones on her ears, listening to music as she waited for the pill stockpile to work its magic, to take her from us. She left a note for Jim, but not one for me. I don't know what her note to him said. I imagine it said "Good-bye" and "I love you" and "Thank you." I hope it did. Her manners were impeccable, and I would not like to think that changed just for a suicide note.

Niecy finishes the last braid, but it's too tight. It hurts. I don't complain. I want to feel the pain, to feel anything other than the rock-hard fullness in my belly. I ate a pounder bag of M&Ms with little help from skinny Niecy, and it might have been sawdust for all the taste my mouth does not savor. Once the fullness in my stomach has subsided to emptiness, I will rub my tongue hard around the inside of the ring until the lip swells. I will taste the blood and feel something again.

I don't know what's the matter with me that Laura could have taken her own life and I have not cried. I don't believe it's real. It's like Laura took her own life, but not really. I expect to climb up to the tree house and find her there waiting for me with a book and a pack of cigarettes, and I will tell her all the drama going on down at the house. *Laura, guess what? The mistress of the house, dead by her own hand—for real and not in some gothic romance novel.*

Now that my hair is finished, I can go outside for a smoke break, find Laura if I try, follow her if I want. I'm not allowed to smoke in the house.

Laura was considerate, and secretive. I don't think

anyone besides me knew she smoked. She asked her own father to give up his smoking habit for her sixteenth birthday present to her. He did. Jim wanted to give her a car.

Braids complete, Niecy sits down on the couch next to my chair. She takes my hands in hers. Her big brown eyes are wet and the smile is gone from her face. I feel her touch but not her warmth. I am immune. Niecy says, "I don't understand. Nobody had more to live for. How could she take her own life? It's like stealing from God."

Laura was like me. Secretive, and an atheist. She did not steal from God. She determined her own destiny, a leader.

I understand why Laura did what she did. I think I'm supposed to be mad at her, but I'm not. I admire her courage. She saw what the world had to offer and said, No thank you. She saw the lies and hypocrisy and violence and hate and meaningless of it all and she chose another path. She won't live to see her grandchildren, but she also won't live to see them suffer.

I pull my hands back from Niecy's. "You're right," I answer. "You don't understand." Niecy has the perfect life. She's pretty and smart, lives in a beautiful home with a loving family. She has a community, and faith. Laura had those things too, but she wanted not to need them. I have none of those things, but I don't miss them either.

I do miss Laura. I miss her so much already and it's only been three days. I still think she's away on a trip and will return home at any moment, loaded with presents for me from a place like Italy or Venezuela or New Zealand. Jim used to invite me on their trips, safe in the knowledge that I would refuse. I am a D.C. girl. I don't want to go anywhere. And I don't want to be his charity case any more than my living circumstances make necessary.

How will I sustain the rest of my life missing Laura, every waking moment of every day of every year, forever? She went away in the past, but she always came back.

I want to be sick.

Niecy leans over to give me a hug whether I like it or not. I am stiff in her embrace. She says, "Don't be like that. Today is not the day to be Miles." She kisses my cheek and turns away from me to leave. Her mom and my mom are waiting for her at Jim's house to help prepare for the arrival of guests. Mourners.

"Thank you," I whisper, but Niecy is already gone.

When is the day to be Miles?

I stare at the commercial on the television. On the screen, a cartoon teddy bear jumps in the air, landing in a snuggly blanket. YAY! Fabric softener!

Nothing's wrong with the world—go out and shop!

I don't believe in anything, especially today.

The 'Nam

BACK IN THE 'NAM, IT'S A STEAMY JUNE DAY, A PROMISE of the oppressive, dangerous summer to come. The temperature is over a hundred degrees. Our nerves are at boiling point. The killing fields wait to implode.

Laura and I hide out in the tree house. Charlie surrounds us, but with the lush summer bloom of the trees outside the window, shrouding us in leaves and brush, Charlie is unaware. Still, we don't dare light a cigarette. One false move, one smoke signal sent into the sky, and we will be shipped home in body bags.

"Once upon a time," Laura whispers to me, "Bravo Company got lost in the Mekong Delta."

It's too late. Charlie has found us, snipping through the brush with his gardener's hedges. He peers at us through the tree house window. "Hi, girls!" he chirps.

Game over. The 'Nam is no fun to play when the real Vietnam vet, Jim's gardener and pet rehabilitation project the year we were thirteen, sits outside the window on a ladder.

"Miles!" I hear the grating voice but choose to ignore it.

The steamy heat of the 'Nam has infiltrated my bedroom. Beads of sweat gush down my face, epithets of frustration and panic. I can't get the zipper at the back of my black dress to close. Last week it went up fine. The M&Ms reconnaissance mission has already swelled me.

Outside my open bedroom window, I hear people arriving for the funeral service. Through the dense trees, they won't notice the carriage house sitting near to the side street at the back of Jim's property, over the imposing fence, through the garden, past the pool. They've discovered the back-alley street with the secret parking spaces, but that thrill will quickly be forgotten as they walk around to the main street, where they will be blinded by the magnificence of the big manor house.

I watch the procession of elegance from my bedroom window as the mourners walk on the ancient cobblestones outside. They're the politicians, socialites, and gay elite who populate Jim's Georgetown world, and over the click of their fine shoe heels, I hear them talking to each other, bracing themselves for the afternoon to come. They're tossing out phrases like "Such a tragedy" and "Senseless loss" and "That poor man." I do not once hear them utter the solitary word that is the real truth. *Suicide.*

"MILES!"

I loosen the dress from my arms and let the top half hang from my waist. I spray another layer of antiperspirant into the pits. Then I put my arms back into the dress and open my bedroom door.

"Can you zip this up in the back for me?" I ask my mother.

"Miles! Did you hear me knocking at your door? Could you please be a little more cooperative, at least today?"

I'll be cooperative enough to let her zip me up. I step over to where she stands at the door. She knows better than to walk all the way in without an invitation.

"Turn around," Mel says. I stand with my back to her. "Deep breath, suck it in. This dress does not want to close." I take a deep inhale, knowing the question that will come next, but still hoping for a pardon. No such luck. "Do you have anything else to wear? Something in a bigger size? I can't get the zipper up all the way to the neck."

"Don't bother." My braids and beads will cover the back. No one will know. My body is ever-expanding, like the universe, but my hair is long, like Laura's.

I have always been the charity girl in the carriage house, content to play the role of sidekick to the princess in the big house, her fat shadow. Now who will I be?

"Jamal and Niecy's mother is in the living room. She wants to talk with you before the funeral service." Mel tugs on a bead at the end of one of my cornrows. "You look very pretty." She has to turn outside the door to allow me room to pass. "Be polite," she warns.

I'm always polite to Dr. Turner. She's not my mother.

I try to walk away toward the living room, but Mel's hand latches on to my own, to hold me back from leaving her sight before she's finished.

I shake her hand loose. "What?"

Her face is gray and hard, jutted in grief, at odds with the harsh noon sun streaming through the hall window. The sun's warmth and brightness feel like a direct laser link to, or from, God. The light's strength is like God is playing a joke on us today. *Hah hah, we've got Laura now, she's all ours.*

I look at Mel's face, which appears to have aged a decade almost overnight, and I know that today I will not be on the receiving end of the When Are You Going to Lose Fifty Pounds and Be Beautiful Like Laura speech. Today I am on the receiving end of my mother's I Buried My Brother and Now My Niece, Both Suicides, face. Her vacant expression tells me that she and I share at least one emotion in common, in the form of a question: How are we supposed to go on?

Poor Mel. She wants comfort, to connect. She should have gotten a Niecy brand of daughter, one who doles out hugs, springs Hallmark sentiments, turns to her in joy and in sorrow. Not a daughter who wants to be left alone with a book, who doesn't want to be touched, who is incapable of love.

She says, "I talked with Paul on the phone this morning. I told him maybe we should reconsider the summer plans. Do you need me to stay here?"

Mel's classic at word-dodging. I know this because I don't know much about anything, except words. Her real question is, *Do you want me to stay?*

She's been on-off with this Paul guy for years; their relationship survives because of the long distance. She's a painter who gets by as a waitress in D.C., he's a sculptor who gets by as an egotistical success story in London. He often travels through D.C. when selling to galleries, and she stays with him in England during the summers when she can enlist my father to make special guest appearances in the role of temporary chaperone at the carriage house.

I have no interest in Paul, or in London. I like to be left behind. It's what I know.

If I were a writer crafting my mother for a story, I would speculate that for Mel, procreation was something she thought she was supposed to do—biological imperative and all—but the whole deal turns out to have been a big disappointment to her, like motherhood was for Scarlett O'Hara in *Gone with the Wind*. The book version of Scarlett loved her pretty daughter Bonnie, but Wade and Ella, her other two kids, the ones who didn't show up in the movie, were runts like me, nuisances—easily written out. My author self might speculate that Mel's like Scarlett, a flawed character with the potential to be a full one—if I took the time to flesh her out. But she's my mom and not a literary character. I can't be bothered. I'd rather read about Scarlett.

I am at least a good enough daughter not to answer Mel's question truthfully. No, I don't *need* you here. I don't *want* you here either. I'm fine by myself. In fact, I prefer it. And please, no need to enlist my father for parent duty again. The only thing Buddy's good for is fixing appliances. The air-conditioning in the carriage house works fine, despite the sweat dampening the fabric of my black dress, despite the open window of my bedroom letting all the cool air out so that I can feel the stifling hot air. Suffer.

"You should go to England," I tell my mother, walking away. "I'm fine."

I'm not fine. Soon, the tears will come. I can sense them building in the pit of my stomach, coating the belly full of candy. They will come when I am alone in the dark, in my own bed, with no one to comfort me. I will mourn Laura then, in private. A Category 5 hurricane is building in my heart and soul, but right now it's offshore, waiting to make landfall, waiting to crush me. I will stock up on supplies beforehand, cigarettes and novels and candy, maybe a glow stick to shine on the walls, to ferret out Laura's ghost.

Code

DR. TURNER SITS ON THE LIVING ROOM SOFA, WEARING an elegant black suit, her legs crossed in executive high school principal pose. To look at her is to see the face of upper-middle-class D.C.—the Gold Coast, African American version. There's her fine, tailored suit. Her lovely mocha skin and perfectly coiffed hair. Her iron will and tender brown eyes. When she speaks, it's like hearing the Future Ph.D. Educator version of her daughter Niecy. "I wanted to check in on you before the service. How are you hanging in there, honey?" Only because she's my best friend's mother am I exempt, at least today, from the frown she reserves for the C- students at her school who are wasting their potential. "Is there anything we can do for you?"

Don't let Jamal leave D.C. for college in Atlanta this fall. Please. I'll have no one left.

"I'm fine," I mumble.

Like Dr. Turner hasn't done enough already. She's been at Jim's house round the clock since hearing the news, overseeing funeral arrangements and food preparation, comforting Jim. Those two go way back. Their committees are the political past, present and future of D.C.'s drive for home rule, to make the District an official State of the Union.

Dr. Turner stands up from the sofa and, like Niecy, reaches to smother me in a hug, whether I like it or not. I do feel her warmth, even through the air-conditioning and my sweaty clothes. She says, "When all this is over, you and I are going to sit down and have a talk. Understand? About this situation, about your schoolwork, your future . . ." Her voice drags off as she chokes up. When she regains her composure, she adds, "I'm going to let you slide through this last week of school, but don't think you and I will not be addressing the serious issue of your academic performance, and your future, once we get through this."

You'd think it would be a perk for your best friend's mother to also be your high school principal, but it's not. I won't bother dropping in the news that I intend to drop out. *No need for a future discussion about my academic performance, Dr. Turner. 'Cuz I ain't goin' back.*

"Miles, I want you to know that the guest room at our house is all yours this summer, whenever you want or need it. We're here for you. All you have to do is let me know when to come by to get you. I have plenty of D.C. statehood committee work to keep you busy, to keep your mind engaged on something hopeful rather than all this sadness, if I can tempt you?"

The offer tempts not. I might agree with her political platform, but I will never spend the night in their family's guest room, despite the many invitations. Me in one room, Jamal sleeping in the next room, playing Morse code against the wall divide? Forget about it. Jamal may BFF love me, but he doesn't understand my secret code like Laura did. He couldn't handle it if he did.

"I'll think about it," I say. I already have. *No.* "Thank you for the offer."

As Dr. Turner leaves to go back to the main house, Mel takes her place standing in front of me. She wants me to fall apart in her arms, I know it. "How *are* you hanging in there, honey?" Mel asks, imitating Dr. Turner's inflection. "Maternal" and "instinct" are not two words that necessarily go together for Mel, but she learns by example from Dr. Turner, on occasion.

I'm about to tell her I'm fine, again, but she falls apart instead, bursting into tears, grabbing my plus-size self to her compact frame. She sobs, "I don't know how I'm going to get through this. I can't believe this is happening to me again."

Because that's what Laura's death is all about—Mel.

I say, "You'll feel better when you get to London. You love it there. You thrive there, you always say."

I'll feel better when she gets to London, when I can have the house to myself, when I can sleep through half the day, chain-smoke, read as many paperback novels and engage in as little human interaction as possible, without her complaint. Then I will figure out how I will make it through the rest of my life missing Laura.

Mel nods, sniffs onto my shoulder. "You're tougher than me, Miles. You'll be okay once I'm gone." I know she's trying to convince herself, not me, that it's okay for her to go. She lifts her head from my shoulder and faces me, gently rubbing her hand along my double chin. "You know how much I love you, right?"

Sure I do. But what's love got to do with it?

High Mourning

I AM HIGH.

As the Jesuit priest, a theology professor and long-time friend of Jim's from the university, orates about God offering the opportunity for repentance in ways we do not know or comprehend, I swear I hear Laura laughing. She's as high as me, only her high is a physical instead of mental space. She's nestled inside a shelf at the top of the fifteen-foot, custom-built bookcase in the library room of Jim's house, over the shelf of leather-bound Shakespeare volumes. She has a gleam in her blue eyes and a book on her lap. I think she's reading a Dan Brown. Rebel! She smiles down at me where I'm sitting in a foldout wooden chair at the back row of seats set up for her funeral service.

A gay father and lapsed Catholic plus a daughter's suicide have equaled no church gathering. But I respect that Jim chose to hold the service in Laura's favorite room in this house, the one without the portraits of Revolutionary generals and their sallow-skinned wives, the one without the framed pictures of presidents and ambassadors who have dined here, the one without the Renaissance tapestries, Oriental vases, and Persian rugs. This is where Laura would want us to be, in the one room that's all about the imagination and not about the exquisite old-money taste. The furniture has been cleared for the service, replaced with aisles of chairs, bathed in the bright light that refuses to subside even on this dark day. What remains are the bookcases that stand for walls, holding the room up with what must be thousands of volumes. Sliding ladders run across the width of the bookcases, our favored amusement park rides when Laura and I were little.

Only I can see her smile. Only I can hear her laugh. "Repentance?" Laura calls down to me. "For whom?"

For these people, I mouth at her, gesturing to the mourners sitting around me. Repent, so that they can feel better. Repent, so they don't have to wonder why. What was Laura's deep, dark secret that compelled her to take her own life?

Only Laura and I know. She carried no deep, dark secret. No secret love affair gone wrong, no acts of shame or hate by or upon her, no heinous crime she needed to hide. She did not kill herself as a means of escaping something. She simply chose not to live. There's a difference. I understand that difference because she and I are the same. We want the same things. She blazes the trail for us, fearless of the unknown, while I cling to the safe and familiar, to living.

I look around at the mourners, truly a rainbow coalition of faces that only Jim could assemble. There are the Congressmen, diplomats and socialites who are Jim's Georgetown neighbors, corporate representatives from the many companies on which Jim serves as a board member, and a solid turnout of African American faces, D.C. people who are Jim's friends from the many civic organizations he belongs to; D.C. may be 70 percent black, but Georgetown gatherings don't necessarily reflect that. I see a small group of student and teacher representatives from the LGBT-youth high school that Jim funds, and an army of pretty white girls from Laura's posh private girls' school. The private-school girls are straight-haired, skinny fashionista clones who look like their every mood is accessorized; today their lip gloss is in the shade of Sad.

I can't look at Jim. To look into his gray eyes and see his suffering, to acknowledge it, would crash me down from this high. I will not be denied. I am not denied. Right now I am surrounded by faces marked with tears and stoicism, but I feel great. Powerful. Perfect.

When I came into this house and saw the somber people gathered, I could not absorb their grief, share it. I immediately darted up to Laura's room. I found her secret stash, no problem. I'm sure she left the stash behind for me. Taped inside the hollow underbelly of her box-spring mattress, I liberated and took as my inheritance her plastic baggie of Oxys and

Percs and Vikes, some purchased illicitly, but most pro-
cured blatantly, from prescriptions left behind by aching
houseguests or depressed live-in maids. I found the one
Oxy20 in the whole bag. I know she saved it for me.
Because a single crushed Oxy equals a dosage of several
Percs, and bestows upon its (ab)user a high that's just too
rapturous; Laura and I considered too deep an attachment to Oxys beneath us. We saved them for Special
Occasions Only. Laura must have known I'd need to
be Special Occasion uplifted today, but not 40-high. I
had just enough time to remove the time-release outer
coating from the pill. I crushed, I snorted, I conquered. I
returned downstairs right as the service began.

Professor Jesuit intones, "We pray for the forgiveness
of the deceased and the comfort of mourners. We ask
that God will reward our faith on the day when all will
be made new again."

What can be made new again if Laura is not here to
experience it?

Professor Jesuit rambles on about God and forgiveness, but I am not bored. I am floating through time and
space, watching a beautiful movie of Laura's and my lives
together. We are six, holding hands across the swings as
Jim and Mel, behind us, push us higher and higher, sun-
light bursting through our movements. We are eleven,
reading *Forever* aloud to one another in her bedroom on a
snow day, giggling. We are fourteen, floating side by side
on rafts at the lake under a cloudy sky, at a distance from
the other summer campers so we can sneak a smoke.

We are seventeen, high up in the tree house, high on Percs, riding out a rainstorm, content to fall together into silent, sweet lethargy, our bodies gliding away from us as our minds settle into emptiness. We own the world and nothing can go wrong.

In our beautiful movie, I can edit out the scenes where I missed that something was wrong with Laura. She knew the movie was ending long before I did. That's why she came back to me this spring. She was saying good-bye.

I am warm and I am cold and I am completely relaxed. I float down from the movie to scratch my stomach. Oxys and Percs make me itch, and I neglected to take a Benadryl to offset the histamine release from the pharm. I scratch my jelly belly in circles, hard and soft, hard and soft. It's a game.

Why does everyone here look so sad? I'm sure they're looking at me strangely. Am I smiling? I think I am but I can't feel my own face. I only feel the happy surging through my veins.

Jamal, sitting next to me, must know I am high. He grabs my hand that's moved to scratch my arm. He clamps our joined hands in the space between our thighs, to keep my hand still, locked in his. I turn my neck to look at his face—dark and beautiful, just like my movie—and see he's shaking his head at me, a warning. Now I feel my face again. It's alive. The corners of my lips turn down, out of the smile. Jamal squeezes my hand. I did good. Much better.

I sit calmly through the remainder of the service,

God redemption forgiveness, tingly floaty tingly floaty, inthenameofthefatherthesonandtheholyghost, hot cold hot cold, Jesus Christ eternal life, happy happy happy.

Laura Laura Laura. Share this with me.

The Cookies Are Divine

WE HAVE NO BODY TO VIEW, NO PROCESSIONAL TRIP TO A cemetery. Laura always planned things through, and that didn't change with her death. She asked for cremation and no burial. She who had everything was at heart a minimalist.

Instead, we have cookies after the service. The dining room is set up with a large buffet of catered food— light salads, polite sandwiches with the bread crusts cut off and cucumbers inside, the *edamame* Laura loved to nibble, set out in the beautiful bowls she brought back from Japan. No one appears to be eating much besides the sweets. Perhaps when an elderly person dies the mourners can reflect on that person's life with a celebration of food and memories, but that is not the case here. I don't hear anyone talking about Laura, no exchange of smiles and laughter—*Remember that time when she . . . ?* I hear chatter, but it's soft, humble. Or maybe I'm too high

39

to properly distinguish the mourners' conversations over their tea and coffee cups. The spread of food is mostly a waste, but the caffeinated drinks appear to be a hit. I'm not the only person here who wants to jolt away the numb.

And who doesn't love cookies—tray after tray of delicate Italian butter cookies; *ghraybeh*, the Lebanese sugar cookies that were Laura's favorites; and an impressive assortment of homemade sweets contributed by the guests. I sample each variety. All these fancy cookies, but the universal truth remains the same: There is no substitute for the wholesome goodness that is chocolate chip cookies. I can picture the Georgetown society ladies arriving with their Saran-wrapped plates: *Jim. Darling. I'm so sorry about your beloved daughter killing herself. Here are some chocolate chip cookies our cook made. The secret ingredient is cardamom. Delicious, no?*

We stand at opposite corners of the dining room, Jim and me, the two pillars of Laura's life. I feel like I should go over to him, touch him, talk to him, tell him I'm sorry, but I can't. I don't. The food rises high between us, buffering all these people, the fillers of Laura's life. The gathered surround Jim, offering solace, but I remain alone, observing. If Jim notices me at all, I'm sure it's to think, *That weirdo. Maybe now I can finally let her go. There's no more reason for her to stay.*

My feet are lodged to the floor in the remote corner of this expansive room. My head is dizzy and my body wants to sway. I yearn to take a very long nap. I place one hand against the wall to prop me up. I need something or someone to hold me steady. But all I have are cookies.

Professor Jesuit approaches me, looking old and kindly, which I hate. I look down, concentrate on the plate in my hand and the Oxy tingle-buzz coursing through my fingers. I have nothing to say to God's handyman. Although if I did, I might inform him that I've given the matter substantial thought, and I've resigned myself to the possibility that I am doomed to an afterlife of eternal hellfire, and I'm okay with it, really I am. It's not like I even believe in God, but still, I imagine Him and me in a powwow on Judgment Day. Saint Peter or whomever has the day off so God himself is going down the checklist for my entrance to Heaven. He goes: *Well, Miles, you smoked like a chimney and indulged in way too many trans-fatty foods, and for Christ's sake, you were high at your own cousin's funeral, but otherwise, you did all right in life. Didn't hurt anybody but yourself. Paid your taxes. Recycled. Helped little old ladies cross the street. (Didn't you?) But I don't know . . . those snarky comments, that vile cynicism during times of crisis. I'm not so sure I like it.* I will then have to set Him straight. *Hey, Big Guy, get some perspective. Who gave us a world of Holocaust, AIDS, global terrorism, famine, ecological disaster, bigotry, genocide, warfare—shall I keep going down the list? Maybe it's ME who should be judging YOU, and not the other way around. So step aside from those pearly gates to Heaven or Hell, whichever the case may be, bucko. Let me through to Laura. We're not scared of You.*

Professor Jesuit passes me by. Minion.

The cookie plate in my hand mesmerizes me with swirls of color and texture, rainbow sprinkles and cinnamon rays and powdered sugar dust, and I must look up again because the cookies are dizzying me. I raise my eyes from their plate reverie, but my view of the mourners has clouded over, gone mute. My eyes lock with Jim's across the room, and in that flash instant, no one exists in this room besides the two of us. In that brief moment, our eyes remember a shared lifetime of Laura, and I see his chest suddenly heave, trying to contain a sob—he who has remained stoic and gracious throughout the afternoon, comforting all those who are trying to comfort him. It's like electricity passes between us, because I feel the heave in my chest as well, and tears well in my eyes. The plate trembles in my weak fingers and I must look back down again, return to my cookie-plate trance, steady my hand. To hold the moment any longer would mean neither of us could remain in this room, finish this gathering of mourning.

Jim's probably more of a weirdo even than me, in my opinion, but God can take note. I am not without empathy. I know what it is like to be Miles right now, a freak high on sugar and so much more, but I do wonder how it must feel to be Jim in this moment, too. He's a seventy-two-year-old man who marched for civil rights, women's rights, gay rights, but chose to focus the latter part of his life on raising a child. What will the latter-latter part of his life now be? A philanthropist born into extreme privilege because his great-grandfather invented an appliance still used in most First World households, Jim parlayed his wealth and privilege for relatively modest selfish purpose—a grand house, grand trips—while choosing to funnel the bulk of his time and money into activism, into his hometown. And now to have his lifetime of giving come down to this one day. His cherished daughter, his one best accomplishment, took away the fundamental gift he had created for her. Life.

My cookie trance breaks when I am mauled in an embrace by the last person here from whom I would have expected—or wanted—comfort. "It's like it doesn't feel real or something, you know?" Bex, Laura's high school best friend, says to me. Her talents reside on the field hockey field, grunting and running and hitting, so I imagine she can be forgiven her lack of articulation skills. Bex is the person who named me "8 Mile," thinking I didn't know. She didn't even go to the same school as me. Yet the name traveled.

I'll never figure out how a girl like her managed to be invited to five proms this year alone; nor do I understand why at the moment of mutual acknowledgment of our shared person's suicide, this is the thought that occurs to me in relation to Bex. But it's true—she's not even that pretty, yet somehow her shiny white smile on pink dimple cheeks always wins out, despite her plain brown hair and eyes, her curveless, boylike, field hockey body. Bex is a girl who would never understand what it's like to have an 8 Mile butt, because she doesn't even have a butt.

I step out of her arms. I don't want that stick touching me, even if she did love Laura. She's the reason I lost the last few years of Laura—Bex, and he who trails behind her, Jason, Laura's ex-boyfriend. At least he will not try to touch me. Handsome soccer-star boys who just finished their first Ivy League year won't bother trying to comfort a girl like me, heavyweight to his featherweight class.

"Hey," he says to us. He's so blond and handsome, it would almost be intoxicating, if not for his predictable, casual acceptance of it, as if those looks and that privilege were the natural right of any white boy from Woodley Park whose parents are both telegenic political media commentators.

What's there to say back? *Hey? Bummer about that suicide and all, right, dude?*

Laura took us by surprise when she broke up with Jason after New Year's. Now I get it. Laura wanted Jason to understand his freedom to move on. After.

Has Jason ever noticed how much Laura and I look alike? Shave me down a dozen sizes, straighten and dye my hair back to its natural color, take off the goth makeup and give me a fresh-faced cover-girl glow, and I could be Laura. I could be the one to console him. I could envelop him.

But it's Bex who jumps into Jason's arms, pressing her face against his lean chest. What it would be like to be her, open to touch, expecting that anyone would want it from her? She holds on to Jason tightly. In their embrace, I see that soon, their grief could potentially turn to something deeper. Laura wouldn't mind. I do.

I am not without my own knight in shining armor. Jamal has found me again. Not only is he my best friend, he's my psychic; I don't realize I am parched until I see him standing before me, bearing a tall glass of water. "Thought you could use this," he says. He hands me the water and I gulp it right down. He asks Bex, "Weren't you the girl who tutored my sister Niecy in math this year? Seems like I've almost met you about a dozen times." Niecy goes to the same school that Bex and Laura just graduated from. Jamal's a mama's boy; he had no problem going to the charter high school where his mother is the principal, but Niecy, she wanted her own path, the one with the fancy girls.

Bex loosens herself from Jason's arms and turns to Jamal, appraises him. What's not to admire about the black suit and baby-blue silk tie (for Laura), his caramel eyes and smooth cocoa skin, or the Afro hair he's disciplined into ten braids running the length of his scalp, knotted at the nape of his neck? Jamal must meet Bex's standards. She smiles, momentarily distracted from her grief. "Don't tell me. You're the brother who blasted all the D.C. go-go music from the speakers in his attic room so we had to go to the library to get any studying done in peace? I mean, I like old Chuck Brown and Rare Essence just as much as anybody who grew up here, but Niecy was trying to raise her PSAT score, and you weren't helping."

"You're Rebecca, right? *Seven-up!*" Jamal responds. Bex couldn't know Jamal's way of acknowledging a person he likes is to speak to them in snippets of songs, prefer- ably by Parliament, his favorite funk band from back in the day.

"Everybody calls me Bex. *Ho!*" she sings back. I would not have expected a girl like her to speak in Parliament.

Jamal doesn't date white girls. Why should he, he says, when he lives in Chocolate City, surrounded on every block by the finest-looking flavors of nonvanilla?

I can no longer deny the Oxy, deny the sway gripping my body, throwing me off balance, hurtling me either toward passing out on the floor, or to a good long nap. Jamal sees it, catches me before I fall. His palm presses against the heavy folds of my arm, warming me.

"Go home and sleep it off." He leans over to whisper in my ear, and my body tingles all over again in anticipa- tion of our private exchange, free of Bex's ears. "This is so not cool today, Miles."

Who's he to judge?

I expect Jamal to take my hand and walk me home to the carriage house, which he would do if we'd whiled away an afternoon down by the canal, sharing a joint. Instead, his hand that's holding me up gently pushes me away, to regain my own balance. His attention turns to Bex, nonnegotiable, nonreturnable.

Teenagers. So fickle.

I am still high, but crashing down.

Back in the Day

THE GAME JAMAL AND I PLAYED THE LAST FEW SUMMERS was this: The Great Cake Con.

Last day of school. Jamal's finished signing everyone's yearbooks, and I've finished patiently standing behind him while no one asks me to sign theirs.

We pick a fancy pastry shop in a yuppie neighborhood like Dupont Circle or Foggy Bottom. We sprint there after the final bell rings in our summer freedom. We admire the concoctions in the glass cases, the tortes and pies, the buttercream and mocha fillings, the mousse cakes and rum cakes and shortcakes and Black Forest cakes, oh my.

Our mouths appropriately salivating, Jamal asks to speak with the store manager. He explains that we're getting married next week. Eloping, actually. Maryland's just a hop-skip-and-jump away, right? We don't need Vegas. The Chesapeake'll do us fine. We're . . . pause as

Jamal smiles bashfully down at my generous stomach as I arch my back to jut the belly out further . . . in the family way, and we don't want to wait to make this about-to-be family legal. We're gonna tell our folks when we get back from the justice of the peace. Sure, we're young, but we're crazy in love. Figure, we'll lay out a spread of cake so grand, the folks'll be too buzzed on the cake to get angry over our little accident who's surely gonna bring joy to their old ages. But . . . sir or ma'am, could you help us out here? 'Cuz we need to sample the cakes, but we don't have the cash to try each one. We're going to break the bank on the final product, once we've picked the perfect cake. It's gonna be a big moment. The cake has to be just right. Naw, we don't have a fancy wedding planner to arrange cake samplings—what, you kidding?

The act, of course, is preposterous. A dapper, fine-looking brother choosing a faux goth, pale sister, the extra with too much extra, to romance-mate? Only on a play date. Yet, as play-for-cake, the act works. With any-body else, we'd be kicked out of the establishment after the first bashful smile. But Jamal, he can pull it off. No one can turn down that honest face and sugar smile. He's never not sincere—even when he's acting. His heart's all the way in it.

Jamal's parents have groomed him his whole life to follow in their footsteps—university at his father's alma mater, Morehouse College in Atlanta, the all-black elite men's school (his mother went to the women's college, Spelman, across the way), then back to D.C. and a career in law and D.C. politics. I think they've pegged Jamal into the wrong plan. Jamal should be lighting up the stage and screen, far from home. But I like his parents' design schematic better. It means he'll eventually have to return to D.C., to me. I'm not going anywhere.

We have our cake and eat it, too.

After the posh bakery charade, we go to the local supermarket chain, Giant Food, to celebrate the con. Jamal spins me for a slow dance in the freezer aisle before dipping me down low, pressing into my back with one hand as he opens the freezer door with his other hand.

I'm uncomfortable with anyone touching my rolls of flesh, so as a rule, I don't dance. But I will with Jamal. Especially for more cake.

"M'lady," Jamal sings into my ear.

"Good sir," I announce back into his. "Another year, another jive act. Mayhap thee should be congratu-funk-ing-lated."

I stand tall out of his dip and glance into the freezer case. I choose the kind of generic sheet cake Laura and I always liked best for our birthdays—chocolate with white frosting, and a plastic clown face jutted into the middle. Jamal and I will bring the sheet cake home to Laura, to eat inside the tree house. We'll dig into it with forks, not bothering to cut slices. We'll eat around the edges, the heaviest frosting parts, until only the carcass of the cake remains, with the maniacal clown in the middle.

Maybe we'll all share a joint after.

The annual cake con heralds summer. Laura will

leave on holiday with Jim soon enough. Jamal will attend
some precollege summer enrichment program his parents
have chosen for him. I will pass the summer smoking and
reading books and missing them even when they're right
there with me.

They dessert me before deserting me.

This year there is no last day of school. No game. No
cake. There is no Laura to come home to.

French Gray Goodness

I SHOULD PROBABLY LIVE IN FRANCE WHERE MY understanding is that it's socially acceptable to wear all black and chain smoke. I will have to starve myself for a few months before I go. I don't think they like fat people or Americans there. But I can lose the weight and pass myself off as Canadian. I will get along fine in France, *mais oui*, and *eh*? I will smoke instead of eat the beautiful pastries, and I will drink lots of coffee. Eventually I will have so many toxins filling my body I won't be able to feel anything at all. That's okay in France.

In the shaded nook of garden behind Jim's house, I have my own private France. Here I can sit on a carved wooden bench under the giant oak tree with the full green branches, protected by the tree house situated over my head. I can smoke to my heart's content, fill my lungs with tar, course my body with nicotine. I can pretend I am sitting outside the Louvre or Versailles or any of those famous France places that have lush, expansive gardens, and where people are allowed to smoke in public establishments without the antismoking Gestapo charging in to ruin their peaceful time. Here in my own private garden, I can be a world away from D.C., waiting to meet up with Laura, to share secret smokes up in the tree house, to talk about first periods, boy crushes, the tyrannical social hierarchy system of the middle school playground.

The garden behind the big house on Jim's property is no rival to the famous gardens at Dumbarton Oaks, the historic property nearby that anchors Georgetown's royal marriage of architecture to landscape. The garden here is haphazard rather than serene, interesting instead of stunning. In the long, wide yard between the main house and the carriage house there are marble fountain sculptures, roses and magnolia in June bloom, honeysuckle randomly sprouting around the hedges, a mosaic-lined swimming pool at the far back side near the carriage house and under the tall, tall trees separating the garden from the street, but there's no method to the madness. It's as if no real thought or plan went into the lush beauty—stuff was just put there, and nature, and D.C., did the rest.

I like it back here. It's probably better than France. No one will bother me or talk to me in a foreign language and I don't have to pretend to care about ice hockey.

The garden's vibrant colors—daisy yellows, violet blues, fuchsia pinks—today appear to me to have melded into one murky color: gray. Everything looks the same. It used to be I could sit back here and almost taste the deep greens of the swamp climate trees and grass. This morning the garden has no taste, no color. I don't even savor the cigarette I am smoking. I breathe in tar, exhale smoke, taste only gray.

The humidity reminds me: I am not in France. The summer air is heavy and lazy, like me. Strands of curls lock onto the wet on my face. I took out the cornrows this morning, one week after the funeral. I washed my hair but the long, frizzy mane will take hours to dry in this wet D.C. air. I figure I've got at least half a pack of cigarettes to go before my hair dries and Jamal stops by to walk me to work. I light another smoke and return to my book—*Sisterhood of Spies: The Women of the OSS*, about American female secret agents during World War II. When we were little, WWII spygirls was one of Laura's and my favorite games up in the tree house.

"Mind if I join you?"

I am so lost in my gray smoke clouds and gray pages that I did not notice Jim approaching my cigarette perch. I put down my book and see that he, too, looks gray, and not just because of the gray chinos and gray polo shirt he wears, or the gray hair and eyebrows that once shined rusty blond, long before Laura changed the color spectrum of his life.

He asks a simple question, yet it strikes me as funny. Since I started high school, it's like there's been this implicit understanding between Jim and me not to engage one another in conversation. I don't know how that happened. It just did. And now, completely casual, as if my teen years haven't gone by with almost no spoken words between us: *Mind if I join you?*

Code-Name Cynthia is nekkid with her lover inside the French Embassy, waiting for her opportunity to steal secrets of occupied France from the embassy safe. But whatever. "Sure," I say to Jim. He does own the garden, after all. What am I going to say? *Go away, my book's at a really good part?*

"Got a cigarette you can spare?" I eye him suspiciously and he adds, "I think under the circumstances I can be forgiven for picking up smoking again. And don't look so concerned. You will not be the enabler of my downfall. I started back up last week but ran out while I was sleepless last night. I haven't yet had a chance to replenish the supply. Only a few days back on smoking and already, the morning nicotine cravings have set in. Goodness, the price of cigarettes went up in the years since I last smoked!"

Goodness. What a queer word, I think. Not gay, but wrong—a word that's meaningless now, a bygone word from a bygone era, from Code-Name Cynthia's time, as bygone as the word "bygone."

I open the Marlboro box and shake it, extending a cigarette up for Jim to take. He sits down next to me on the bench and lights up. I thought I remembered him as a Virginia Slims man. Lapsed smokers are rarely brand loyal. But I see Jim has resurrected his old Tiffany silver lighter with his initials engraved on it, a gift from a partner from long ago, when same-sex lovers had to stay in the closet but chain-smoking on crowded airplanes and in movie theaters was totally fine, even encouraged. Secondhand smoke was clearly less dangerous than two men sharing the gift of a public kiss, in goodness's bygone time.

We smoke together, silent. I'm sure he's here to bring up the issue I know is forthcoming: my departure from this property. Mel promised me as much before she left for England. *Miles, if recent events have taught you anything, it should be that now is the time for you to take charge of your life. Stop smoking, already, and stop treating your body like a dumping ground for junk food. And you're almost eighteen. You're grown up, almost an adult, and with Laura gone, surely you realize we can't stay here at Jim's forever. My heart is broken. Maybe now's the time for me to seriously consider a permanent move to England with Paul? You've got the summer to start thinking about what you want to do after you finish school. We have to move on and out eventually, I guess. Right, honey?*

When Jim finally speaks, about half a cig down, it's to ask this: "Aren't you hot wearing all that black in this heat? It must be ninety degrees with 90 percent humidity out here." This kind of question is why I avoid conversation with him. He is judging me, and I suspect his verdict on me is always the same: white trash. Sweaty and pudgy, doesn't know how to dress properly.

"I'm fine," I say. These words have become like a mantra spewing from my mouth. Storm update from

Accu-Miles Weather Center: The Category 5 hurricane downgraded to a tropical storm some time between the funeral service and Mel's departure. Low clouds still hover over me when I sleep—*if* I sleep, misting my eyes and sending chills through my body alone in bed at night, but the full-scale rage has yet to come ashore. But it's still early in the season.

I have Laura's leftover bag of goodies to tide me over in the meantime. Half a hydro eases me into slumber, but the half is not so gram-deep I can't wake up in the morning. Smooth.

I'm only a full-on Perc or Oxy junkie for special occasions, like quality time with Laura, or after suicides and during funerals. I can walk away any time. That doesn't mean I don't deserve a little generic half-treat at night when I can't sleep.

I want to distract Jim from my impending eviction, so my question for him is this: "Aren't you going away this summer?"

Rich people don't languish through D.C. summers. They go to Martha's Vineyard and Nantucket, the Outer Banks of North Carolina, little Georgia sea islands, or to France for real.

Jim takes a drag, exhales. "Don't have the heart for travel right now."

In our resumed silence, the real question hangs in the thick air between us: *How are we going to make it through this summer, without her?*

In my childhood, summer *was* Laura. Summer was overnight camp with shared bunk beds, day trips down the Chesapeake, zoo visits, roller-coaster rides, miniature golf, and ice-cream cones. In the summer, I had Laura all to myself. We were our own unit, separated from her school friends—and my lack of them.

Jim finishes his cigarette and throws it on the ground, stubs it out with his foot. I pick up the discarded butt from the ground, then reach for the glass ashtray tucked away behind my back, already filled with a half dozen morning butts. I add his discarded cigarette to the ashtray pile. "No need to litter this beautiful garden," I scold.

He laughs, which is a relief. Words exit too quickly from my mouth. I must train myself to think before tossing out comments to someone who shall determine how long I'll have a roof over my head.

Laura used to make him laugh, performing reenactments of scenes from Jim's favorite old movies, strutting around the family room like Rita Hayworth, or lodging water balloons at him when he was back here in the garden sneaking a smoke despite his ongoing vow to quit since her infancy. I could never fill her void.

More than I'm hoping Jim has not joined me to announce my eviction, I'm hoping he's not here to talk with me about Laura. I'm not ready to deal. For now, all I can do is go on. Smoke. Hunger.

"Is your dad here yet?" Jim asks.

"Nope. Buddy always promises to get here before Mel leaves, but he never does. But you know I'm fine on my own."

"Do I?"

Jamal's early arrival saves me from answering Jim's question. Jamal never fails to know when I need him.

Jamal's arrival can be heard before we can see him standing at the doorway to the carriage house. He's got jumbo earphones on his head, although the high bush of Jamal's newly unbraided Afro hair obscures them. His audio player must be at full blast if I can hear it so distinctly from my garden perch a few yards away. Old school hip-hop meets Broadway musical from Jamal's headphones, with some rapper riffing on how it's a hard knock life.

If it weren't for Jamal, I would probably not know or recognize any form of popular music—yet another sign that I am a freak and a failure as a teenager. I will listen to music with Jamal, but rarely on my own. Words are better experienced through sight rather than sound. What's to hear? It seems to me that most songs are about love—wanting it, finding it, losing it—all pointless and irrelevant to a size-challenged listener who's never been kissed or gone on a single date. The musical message is the same as those Jane Austen books I hate and refuse to hand-sell at the bookstore. Why did that old girl have to start that Get A Man mythology of literature, anyway? Boring boring boring, a waste of time. I'd rather absorb the bleakness of Burroughs or Bukowski, or even the sophisticated, mean-spirited wit of Dorothy Parker, rather than choke down the false promises of Austen and her descendants.

The fundamental lesson from the Fat Girl's Guide to Surviving Popular Culture, besides the obvious one—*never* open up a fashion/beauty magazine dedicated to Hate Your Body But Learn to Pleasure Your Man principles—has got to be to avoid that Jane Austen lady's books and all the movies her books have inspired. Think about it. In real life, men who look like Hugh Grant and Colin Firth do not have punching matches over a "fat" girl (who's not even fat). Hot men wearing breeches may eventually go for the interesting girl, but only if she's a stick-figure Gwyneth. I've issued a complete ban on these books and their movies from my life. I don't like being lied to.

"Guess I'd better go," I tell Jim. I take one cigarette from my pack for the walk to the bookstore and hand over the remaining box of smokes to him. I can afford to be generous; I've got a carton in my room and a part-time bookstore job to pay for the supply. I place the leftover cigarette in my mouth, expecting Jim to light it for me with bygone's lighter, but he only blankly stares at me—or, rather, through me. He must also see gray these days.

"Thanks," he says. "Is there anything you need?"

"I'm fine," I repeat.

"Well, if you do need anything . . ." I almost, *almost*, finish the sentence for him, instinctively remembering what he always said to Laura instead of "good-bye," but for once I manage to rein in my mouth, and Jim speaks the words for himself: "You know where to find me."

I light my own cigarette. Matches.

"Thanks," I say. I walk away, toward Jamal.

I won't be looking.

Virginia Is for Haters

JAMAL THINKS I SHOULD PLAY HOOKY FROM WORK AND take an adventure with him. We could make like George and Martha Washington and hang out in Old Town Alexandria, browse the art galleries and record stores, talk in Ye Olde Jivespeak that only the two of us understand. *Why, Miss Miles, I declare, your reputation is in danger of tarnation with that there interplanetary funky butt jivestep yo' fine self is struttin' down this alleyway. Why, Mastah Jamal, thee gots to be funked up to think me capable of funky butt. Mayhap thee has been imbibing of the cider troth too much?*

Mama's pride and joy heads off to Daddy's alma mater in the fall, so I should be taking this opportunity for time with Jamal before he leaves for Morehouse in Atlanta. But Jamal must really be smoking some funky stuff not to remember that I don't care to hang out in Alexandria, not even for Ye Olde Jivespeak.

I hate Virginia. Mostly for vague reasons like the

whole state just *bugs* me, but for some valid, specific ones too. There's the state's across-the-river association with D.C., subjugating it from across the Potomac, sheltering the Pentagon and the CIA, and housing the hordes of transient residents who come from other places to work in D.C., gridlocking the highways and necessitating the building of strip malls and superstores; I swear, the whole of Northern Virginia is one long traffic jam to IKEA. And let's not forget, Virginia is where that General Lee guy came from. Remember him? The general who tried to save the Confederacy so that the fine institution of slavery could be upheld?

"Nope," I tell Jamal as he stands next to me while I unlock the Once upon a Time storefront. "Count me out." I have my principles.

Even if I wanted to, I couldn't skip out on work. The storefront door was tagged with graffiti sometime between yesterday and today, leaving the chestnut-colored door emblazoned with black and purple insignia that I do not understand. I'm less irritated and more fascinated that I will have to spend the first part of my work afternoon cleaning it off the door when I'd otherwise be lost inside one of the store's books.

I wouldn't mind being a graffiti artist, enrolled in a secret revolution fought through symbols and hidden meaning. If I could decipher the graffiti code enough for rudimentary communication, I would answer the "vandals" with my own graffiti message on the store's door, in black spray paint: *Consider this store your safe haven. 8 Mile wants to rap with you. Will not call police on you. Respects your artists' way. Would like to learn your secret language. Any takers?*

"Do you know who did this?" I ask Jamal, pointing to the graffiti.

"That's right, ask the brother, he's sure to know all the colored ones coloring up pristine Georgetown with graffiti."

"Hah-hah. But seriously, do you know? Because I would like to meet these people. Don't you think they're like stealth ninja artists? Ride the Metro through tunnels, look out the window when you're on the track riding over a bridge, and what do you see? Graffiti. Who are these people pulling this off? When? Have you ever seen them? How do they manage to get it into those obscure spots that must require lots of dangerous climbing and dangling in order to get that one perfect paint perch? Don't you want to know?"

"Don't particularly care, and you're dodging the question." We step inside the store. Jamal flips on the lights as I head toward the cleaning supply closet behind the cash register counter. "Sistah Miles, I know from experience that you can be persuaded to ditch this place and come experience the world with me today. So what's it gonna take to make you say yes?"

I have no intention of saying yes—the day is just too gray, despite the hot yellow sun poking through the window shades—but I am curious nonetheless. "Why do you want me to miss work? You score some nice weed?"

"No. And do I have to score some nice weed in order to have an excuse to take you on an adventure?" He smiles at me, big white teeth on a full red mouth of pure sweetness. As his brown eyes catch my own, I almost catch my breath at the vision of him. If he dated white girls and I wasn't a fat one, I would probably be in love with this boy.

"You know that's not true. It's that since . . . you know . . . I just don't feel like going anywhere." I never feel like going anywhere anyway, but historically I have been open to exceptions if the doing something involves getting some part of Jamal's time.

Jamal jumps over the counter to stand next to me. "That's the thing," he says, excited. "That Bex girl, she feels the same. So I thought I could get all of us together and go somewhere—"

"What do you mean, 'that Bex girl'? What, are you friends with her now?"

"Maybe getting to be. I like her. She's cool."

"She's not cool. You know who her dad is?"

"I do. I won't hold it against her. That's not her fault."

How very open-minded of Jamal. His mother is a leading advocate of D.C. home rule, yet he chooses to potentially ally himself with the daughter of one of the District's great enemies. Let's call him Congressman

Same Old White Man. C-man SOWM has served in the House since long before Bex was born. I doubt she even knows what her home state looks like aside from short trips there for photo ops during election years. He regularly declines his party's overtures for him to make a run for Senate, because why should he risk his political clout? The promotion would in fact be more of a demotion, since he'd have to start all over on the other side of the Capitol. Congressman SOWM has been a representative so long, he's an institution in the House, with influence on all the important committees. And he repeatedly uses that influence to thwart D.C., year after year making sure that any legislation that proposes to give power to the very city he calls home never makes it out of committee, much less to the floor of Congress for a real vote.

As if the very fact of an Electoral College that decides our most important election, regardless of the popular vote, was not evidence enough of our forefathers' (that Philly crew of Same Old White Men) tenuous connection to the concept of fairness, the issue of D.C. statehood proves to me that there truly is no justice in this country. The population of D.C. is greater than that of Wyoming, and comparable to that of Vermont, Alaska, North Dakota, and South Dakota. Yet each of those states gets two senators and a handful of congressmen to represent them. D.C. gets nothing besides one token representative to Congress, whose vote means nothing. I appreciate the right of gun-toting, freedom-loving South Dakotans to be represented in Congress, I really do—but shouldn't D.C. residents share that same privilege? Uncle Sam cashes their federal tax payment checks the same as those from all the other states. But I suspect those Same Old White Men who've been ruling the world since Jesus's time wouldn't want D.C., with its majority black population, to have a fair vote in our nation's important decisions. The injustice is that most un-American of principles made legal for the sake of the federal city D.C. harbors: taxation without representation.

I may have gotten a C- in American Government this past term, but that doesn't mean I don't know or care about understanding how the system works. I just don't feel the need to write properly, punctuated—papers: about; it. To me, requiring a born-and-bred D.C. resident to study American Government is like asking a fat person to join a dating service—why bother, when you're going to be ignored, anyway?

Jamal asks, "Is this one of your stupid Virginia-hating things? Because we don't have to go to Alexandria. That was a bad idea."

"It's a D.C. thing."

"Says the girl who won't even get a D.C. driver's license?"

"I'm an environmentalist. I take the bus."

"Then why won't you go and at least get the official photo ID card from the D.C. DMV?" I start to answer, but Jamal holds up his hand to stop me. "I know, I know, you're not going to be subjugated to government profiling so long as the federal government's enslavement of

D.C. persists. I've heard all about it." He looks at me again, trying to figure out why I really can't be persuaded to take a ditch day. When his eyes spark, I know he knows. He dropped a word worse than *Virginia*. "Laura didn't hold Bex's father against Bex. Why should you?"

8 Mile has to be honest. "I just don't like her."

If Mel were here, she would throw her hands up in the air, sigh in frustration, glare at me. But Jamal only laughs and pulls me to him. "Mayhap thee needs to funkify some attitude adjustment? Miss Miles, my extraterrestrial sistah from the scowling masthead mothuh ship, is there anything or anybody you don't hate?"

You.

"I like chocolate." I reach under the counter for my energy supply box. I offer the box of Snickers bars to Jamal.

He shakes his head. "Nope. I'm gonna find that Bex girl and take her on an adventure through the real Chocolate City. No need for Snickers when we can find ourselves some serious sweetness somewhere out in the world. So you just stay here and clean graffiti and read books, because that sounds so much better than what I propose." He looks around the decrepit store, piled with books and magazines—all words, all chaos. "Why do you even care about trying to maintain this store, or showing up here at all? You do realize this store has no customers?"

Exactly.

He holds up his phone behind his back for me to see as he walks out the door. "Holla if you change your mind."

I am alone again but I can feel Laura's presence in the store, guiding me. I will clean the graffiti on the door later this afternoon. Let the neighbors enjoy the door art for a while before it's lost to a scrub brush. Surely the hipster yuppies and rich old fogeys will appreciate the urban artistic expression dignifying the view from the windows of their posh homes.

I step over to the Non-Fiction section instead of tending to cleanup duty. I browse the aisle, looking for today's reading selections. I find them on the American History shelves. The Cold War. The Great Depression. Words and eras to live by.

Sleepless in Not-France

TOO MANY HYDROS AND MY BODY WILL DEVELOP A tolerance, so this jive turkey has decided to go cold turkey. Insomnia, you are mine. I embrace you. I accept you. I smoke through you.

"You again," Jim says. He should apply to become the world's first senior citizen ninja graffiti artist, so stealth is he with his movement. I did not see or hear him approaching my middle-of-the-night spot on the bench under the tree house. The crickets humming and fireflies lighting the black night are more noticeable than he. I certainly didn't expect him. I might not be able to see him at all but for the streetlight shining from behind the oak tree.

He sits down next to me. "Can't sleep?" He lights a cigarette. He's back on Virginia Slims.

"Yeah." I place the ashtray in between us and reach for a fresh Marlboro to put in my mouth. Better than

Snickers, those cigs. Overindulgence in smoking will only lead to cancer and lung disease. No one can see internal maladies like they can obesity.

"Same."

Because now it's real. Laura is not coming back. This has not been a cruel joke. It is fact. She is dead. We may think we see her coming through the front gate, blond and chipper on a cold winter's day, a baby-blue cashmere scarf on her head as she's wrapped inside Jason's tight embrace; we may hope it's her laughing voice on the other end when we pick up the phone, asking for directions to the closest Metro stop because she's lost again; and we may pray for a do-over of that recent day—the ambulance arrived sooner, the stomach pump retched those pills from her body before it was too late. But we know the difference now.

All we have left is nothing.

An unlit cigarette dangles from my mouth. I see the lighter in his hand, and I pause, thinking he will offer me a light. He does not. As always, I'm on my own.

"You really ought to try to quit smoking," Jim says. *So should you, fella. And stick with it this time.* He crosses one leg over the other, takes another drag. "You're so young. If not for your health, think of all the money you'll save. Your money is better spent elsewhere."

Like paying rent elsewhere?

I cross one leg over the other too, but I don't look as elegant in my cotton pj's as Jim does in his silk ones. He looks down at my Chucks and asks, "Is there something written in glow in the dark pen on your shoes?" Jamal painted the words "Sistah Miles" on the canvas parts of my shoes, my own personalized graffiti funk, but I kept the rubber ends at the top for myself, for words written in secret spy ink that's only visible in the dark. Jim's so old and blind he'd never be able to make out what I wrote: *What is wrong with me!*

"Just scribblings," I tell him.

"'Scribblings,'" he repeats, chuckling. "What a Miles word. When you were little you used to invent the funniest stories and words. Do you still do that?"

Yessuh-fo'sho'. "No."

"You should. I always thought you would grow up to be a writer. Dr. Turner tells me you're quite talented. Though apparently your English teacher thinks you . . . I can't recall—what exactly was the complaint?"

"According to the English teacher, not only do I turn in work late and grammatically incorrect, but I 'squander my gifts on sarcasm.' She just got mad that I didn't find the symbolism she wanted me to find in Twentieth-Century African American literature. She thought my 'Fat Like Me' essay made a mockery of her assignment."

"Did it?"

"Kinda."

He chuckles again.

I add, "She said I should have spent more time discussing the books written by black authors instead of modeling my essay on a book by the white guy who went around in blackface so he could understand racism.

If you ask me, the teacher's criticism was its own form of reverse racism." I wonder what adventure Jamal took that Bex girl on today. I ask Jim, "Did you know that back when Bex's dad was a young state senator, he once supported a measure calling for *The Invisible Man* by Ralph Ellison to be banned from the high school reading lists in public schools?"

"I do recall that, now that you mention it. What's your point?"

"No point, really. I just think it's ironic that I should get a C– on a paper legitimately expressing my opinions about a work of literature, when I took the time to read that book and think about it, and that guy tries to ban great works of art, and he's made one of the most powerful members of Congress."

Jim laughs again. Who knew I was so funny? "A valid point. But to be fair, Bex's dad has mellowed over the years. He may appear to lean far right, but I consider him one of the good guys left in the House. A true gentleman, more center right than perhaps he'd like his constituency—or his party—to believe."

"He votes antichoice and against gay marriage. He's the enemy of D.C. home rule. How can you say that?"

"It's not so black-and-white as that. He may spout one opinion publicly, only to sway it otherwise behind closed doors. Progress takes times—and patience. He chooses his battles. Did you know it was a phone call from him that got the building permit I needed to get the old property on Q Street rezoned so it could be converted into the LGBT high school space? Did you know he's his party's primary supporter of foreign aid to Third World nations, helping to combat AIDS, famine, poverty? He makes sure those funds are secure when others would like it allocated to defense. Not all conservatives are the bogeyman, Miles. And look at the daughter he's produced. There's hope for the man yet."

Glass half full people. Hate 'em. WAKE UP!

"I don't agree." I don't know why I suddenly have so much to say. It must be the night's lack of pharmaceutical enhancement in my bloodstream that's turned my inner mute button to Off. Or it's that just thinking about Congressman SOWM has my blood boiling. He is everything wrong with America. He's that GO TEAM RAH RAH RAH, American-flag-pin-on-his suit-lapel, same old white man who orates about liberty and freedom and then authorizes the Pentagon to plunder other nations in the name of "democracy." He's the guy that had to go and make that stupid Bex girl who took away Jamal today.

Or it's that Jim and I are talking around what—and who—is really on our minds.

Jim's on to cigarette number two. He's got a ways to go to catch up to me. "Why don't you agree? Do you really think there's that much difference between liberals and conservatives? In the end, don't you think we all want the same thing: peace and prosperity?"

"Here's the difference. I'm not trying to change them. I'm just saying stay off my body and don't tell me who I can and can't marry."

Apparently I am not only amusing, I am bloody hilarious. Jim guffaws what are probably his first real laughs since Laura left us. "Miles! Of course you're a writer!"

I don't get the joke. "I'm not. I have nothing to write about."

"Of course you don't," he says, dropping the laughter, his voice turning solemn. "You have no opinions you want to express, no feelings you want to share, not a care in the world about anything."

He must have been talking to my mother.

"That's right," I say.

"Okay," he says.

We go on smoking in silence, the cicada filling the void in our conversation. Jim stubs out cigarette number two and reaches for number three. Before lighting it, he turns to me, as if he has something to say, then he thinks better of it. He lights, takes a drag, exhales. He's halfway down the cigarette before he finally speaks up, in a quiet but firm voice. "You understand that she was sick? That she had every possible source of help available to her but her mental state was such that she was just determined to do it no matter what any of us did to try to help her?"

"Yes." I choke a little on the drag I am inhaling. Only I don't really understand. I get that he's telling me that Laura was receiving treatment; I don't understand how she never told me the pain was as bad as it was.

The crickets whisper their encouragement to me. "I'm so sorry," I murmur. *I'm sorry for your loss, for my loss, I'm sorry I didn't know, I didn't reach out, I didn't help her in time. I'm sorry I don't understand how to go on now other than just sitting here like this, smoking and hurting. I'm sorry I'm not even sure I want to go on.*

My spoken words are barely audible over the crickets. But they're said.

I turn a few centimeters away from him on the bench. No need for hugs or reassuring glances to close the moment. Let's just take the sentiment at face value, here in the dark where we can't see it.

Project Disenfranchisement

JAMAL'S SPECIAL NOT FOR HIS SURFACE QUALITIES—HIS nice looks and gifts as a performer. He's special for his open heart. He doesn't discriminate on the basis of color, size, sexuality, or weirdness; he's anybody's friend who wants to be his. I guess this explains why he can tolerate a Friday night out at the movies with a skinny white girl whose father strives to enslave D.C. rather than share a late night walk around the Lincoln Memorial with me, questioning whether Mr. Lincoln really did make the right decision keeping the United States intact. Since they're not so United anymore and maybe separate was the better way to go.

At least I know where to find Jim. Two lost souls with nothing to do other than grieve and smoke, who share nothing besides a dead person, are getting to be codependent regular players in Midnight in the Garden of Talking and Smoking.

Insomniacs Unite! And Discuss! A carton's worth of smoking conversations with Jim the last few nights have resulted in the following revelation: By any reasonable measures, I'm a lucky girl. I was born with the skin color of privilege, grew up without being physically or emotionally abused (he sidesteps the issue of Mel's absence). I live in a free society, and I have a future if I should choose to take it. But according to Jim, I see myself as disenfranchised.

I ask, "What's so wrong with that?" I'll never be one of those people posturing to think or act "outside of the box." I love the box.

Jim says, "Nothing. But understand that's a choice you make. And if you see yourself as so disenfranchised, imagine how others perceive the way in which you reflect yourself?"

I'm not sure what he means but I know it's not good. I determine to prove him wrong. I'll be sure to stay inside the box while I do it, if only to be spiteful.

I'm not sure if we're ready to talk about her but I can't help myself. She never stops being with me. If anything, she's getting to be more so. "Do you think Laura felt disenfranchised?"

He waits a few drags before answering. "I wish I knew what she felt. She didn't share a lot, not even with her doctors, and especially not with me." He speaks in a matter-of-fact tone that must cover deeper hurt; it's got to be down in there, but I would never dare ask a gentleman so polite about the rage underneath the refined veneer he must feel about what his daughter did. "But my understanding from those who treated her is that mostly what Laura felt was pain. It overwhelmed her, isolated her, and she was in constant struggle trying to cover that up. Laura wanted those who loved her to believe she could handle anything. She agreed to take meds for clinical depression mostly to appease me. At least, she claimed to me to be taking the medication. But she never wanted to talk about it."

How come Laura never talked to *me* about it—the person who would "relate" the most? Laura and I were blood. Jim was not. Her crazy was my crazy.

"How long had she been on medication?" It hurts to acknowledge to Jim that I didn't know she was taking antidepressants. Like I failed Laura in not seeing past her beautiful face and kind disposition, to look deeper, inside, to the gnarly, hateful webs that ravaged her mind, body, and soul, to the parts of her I would have understood best, if she'd let me in.

"Since puberty," Jim says, and I want to laugh. Who else but an old fogey would use the word "puberty" in a sentence, completely straight-faced? "But it was as if she felt shame in needing treatment at all, like it was a weakness, despite my constant reassurances to her to the contrary, despite the many times I told her that the brave choice was to accept help rather than deny the pain." He stubs out his cigarette and lights a fresh cigarette. "Miles, will you promise me you'll do something?"

I exhale from my cigarette drag before replying. "No, I will not."

He's bumming smokes off me tonight, so I can afford the impudence. I know where he's going. But just because Jim and I are getting to be garden-smoking cell mates doesn't mean I'm obligated to accept the extraction of self-improvement promises.

Jim shakes his head, lets out that special laugh I seem to bring out of him, the one I would probably think was patronizing coming from anybody else. "Well, please know that if you feel you need help, need to talk to a professional about Laura . . ."

I get it, Laura. I do. Sadness—it's *your* business, not a stranger's.

I am spared from telling Jim "No, thank you" by a thundering bassline coming through the speakers of someone's mama's Saab driving down the back alley behind the garden. Bob Marley wails from the stereo. *Rastaman, live up!*

Jamal. Saving me once again.

The Saab stops at the curb and the stereo sound is lowered long enough for the emission of a signature series of "C'mon already, Miles" honks before the car stereo returns to reggae blast.

Jim sighs. "Go. Tell Jamal he can answer to my neighbors' noise complaints in the morning."

I don't want to go. That Bex girl is probably in the car with Jamal. I remain on the bench, finishing my cigarette.

"Miles, if we don't cut short at least one night smoking back here, we'll both have emphysema before the summer is over." I turn to face him. *Emphysema.* What a cool word to dangle, and so contradictory—all those pretty letters put together to produce one nasty ailment. Well done, Jim.

Challenge accepted. Project Disenfranchisement— start your engines.

Crash Landing

WHEN I APPROACH HIS CAR, JAMAL SMILES AT ME THROUGH the window from his driver's seat. He's the only person in my life I can count on to have this reaction to me. I know not to read too much into his smile. A fat girl should never dare believe an inviting welcome from a guy is exclusive to her, that it indicates any feeling that's not purely platonic. Jamal shares that warmth with everyone.

"What took you so long, Sistah Miles? Can't get a late Friday night truly started without you by my side."

I glare instead of smile back. Bex is indeed sharing the car with Jamal, sitting in the passenger side. My side. Jamal's driver seat is pushed far back to accommodate his long legs, but I step into the car behind him anyway, smushed, rather than get into the backseat behind her.

That's what I'd like to be. Stuffed inside the box.

Bex leans over from the front and offers me a Twizzler from her jumbo-size bag of candy. She's chewing on a single red strand, probably the same strand she's been on since she opened the bag at the theater. I wonder if Jamal notices the licorice bag is still full but their movie must have ended a while ago. "Want one?" she asks me.

I want the whole bag. And a giant box of Milk Duds, too.

"No." I turn my head away from her to look out the window.

Some people just don't know when they're being ignored. Bex adds, "Alrighty, but let me know if you change your mind. We're onto our second Twizzlers bag tonight, so there's plenty to spare if you want some."

I want to be skinny, like you. I want to be in the passenger side seat, next to Jamal.

I bet Jamal ate the first bag himself with no help from her.

"Thanks," I say. I hope she hears my insincerity. I return to my meaningful, silent stare out the window as Bex and Jamal engage in stereo-control flirtation in the front. Through the window glare, I can see them batting each other's hands at the radio dial. They laugh and argue over which song sucks more, the one on the Lite FM station, or the one on the Christian rock station.

Barf.

Boys just turn into unrecognizable creatures around skinny girls.

Here's what I figure (so to speak): If I were truly dedicated to transforming myself into a thin person like Bex, I would go the easy route and starve my way down.

I'm just no good with commitment, that's my problem. I would give anything to be anorexic or bulimic. But I am a failure at that too, C+ effort at best. How do those girls pull it off? Because I can't help myself. I'm always hungry. I like to digest. Sorry.

On the scale of fantasy eating disorders, I'd weigh in with anorexia over bulimia. True, with bulimia you get to binge and taste something—anything, as much as you want. But puking? No way, so not worth the gluttony. With the starvation option, it's *ahhhh . . . niiiiiiiice*, like a wholly-swallowed Percoset gulped down after hearing the news of an unexpected snow day, school cancelled, on the very day you had a Biology midterm you didn't study for. Strictly first class enjoyable. Anorexia has got to feel the same way, first class high off the energy extracted by your mind's ability to deny your body's fundamental cravings. I'm awed. Even the word looks exotic—*anorexia*—like, all Latin-derivative, mysterious and complicated. What looks glamorous about three hateful letters linked together to spell F-A-T? Right. Nothing.

It's possible I could be diagnosed with anorexia envy like some people have penis envy. A bona fide shrink would probably advise: *Miles, you suffer from anorexile envy—one who covets the ability to exile one's body into foodless bliss. Patient, I see that jealousy through all those blubb-o-layers of yours. You look at the gaunt girls and think, "Well done! You made a goal and you stuck with it! Your hair is falling out and your face is gray, but you're in double digits on the scale. Girl, treat yourself—go out and get yourself a man!"*

While Jamal and Bex engage in their stereo-control power struggle, I open the M&M bag stored in my pocket—carefully, quietly, so they won't hear the paper crinkle. I pop some M&Ms into my mouth, letting the candy dissolve in my mouth instead of crunching it with my teeth.

We're driving through Glover Park, a posh area just above Georgetown, which with its sprawling lawns and fancy houses feels more like a Virginia or Maryland suburb than a District neighborhood. The streets are sleepy. I am not. It occurs to me ask, "Where are we going?" Usually with Jamal, I let myself be driven, no questions.

Jamal has no need to answer. The Saab stops in front of a sprawling corner-lot house, and I see we've arrived at the exact place I didn't know I wanted to be, but here Jamal has taken us. It's the place that can undo my current, highly unpleasant state of stone-cold sobriety. Not even Bex's presence is going to deny me the pleasure I know awaits inside.

The tourists who regularly show up at this street corner are right to be confused. Their D.C. spy maps list the location as being a famous "dead-drop" site during the Cold War, where U.S. government turncoats who worked for the CIA or FBI would leave confidential information inside the mailbox on the street, to be picked up in the middle of the night by KGB spies wearing U.S. Postal Service uniforms. But the infamous mailbox no longer stands at this corner, nor does the gothic old Tudor house pictured in the spy history books. The old house was razed several years ago and replaced by a ginormous McMansion that swallows the entire lot, leaving almost no yard space.

The local kids who know the true tourist attraction to be found at this site refer to it as "Crash Landing"—as if a UFO (perhaps missile-guided by some combination of the KGB, CIA, and E.T. at the controls) mistakenly fumbled onto this spot and destroyed it, then quickly constructed a Disney house on the lot to cover up the alien error. Fortunately, because so many tourists use outdated spy maps and books, their regular presence on this block helps distract the police and neighborhood residents from the other stream of regulars—local teenagers who crash-land here to get high.

The concierge of the house is known as Floyd. His real name is long forgotten. The nickname was given to him by stoner kids, in tribute to Floyd's primary musical influence. Floyd simultaneously deals out of his house, and lets the stoner kids crash here. It's like one-stop shopping. In Upper Northwest, Floyd is brand-name famous, like Target.

The Crash Landing house belongs to his parents, but they're high-finance people who travel more than they stay in their own home. Floyd prefers "the simple life" of D.C. His parents reportedly prefer long-term absence rather than be regularly reminded that their twenty-year-old son is the antithesis of the proper preppy sons of their

Glover Park neighbors, a Big Disappointment. I guess it's a situation that works out on both sides, kind of like me and Mel and the Georgetown carriage house versus London. You take your corner of the universe and I'll take mine. Cue that elevator song about the mother and child reunion only being a motion away, and try not to laugh.

When we enter the house, we see the usual suspects, the local private school kids, mostly white, but some brown and yellow diplomatic faces too, the underage rich and privileged who pass their weekends here. They're well on their way to a happy daze of confused. Metal plays in one room, hip-hop in another. TVs show sports channels or soft-core porn, but the constant to each room is the drug paraphernalia—bongs, mirrors and razors, lighters and needles—spread out across the various tables. Beer and vodka bottles sit on every available windowsill (though all the shades are drawn, naturally), and ashtrays are strewn across the carpeting. The house smells of cigarette and pot smoke, of beer and hard alcohol and, wafting down from the upstairs floors, the whiff of sex—or at least what I imagine sex would smell like, kind of sweet and salty and scary.

Good God, I wonder who Floyd pays to clean the place before his parents return to town.

It's like Jamal forgets right away that I'm even there. Jamal takes Bex by the hand and leads her into a den where music videos blare from an overhead TV and gyrating, E-tripped, boy-boy, girl-girl bodies are soul-dancing up close and personal. Now add in Jamal and

Bex, boy-girl, and a matched set completes the room.

I stand in the hallway, mute. Alone.

I realize: I must develop the ability to go the distance rather than just envy it. I must try harder—franchise franchise franchise. Learn to jog five miles a day along the Potomac, even at sun-death high noon during 90 percent humidity. Learn to keep those two fingers down my throat instead of gagging and pulling them out too soon. Learn to live on Diet Cokes and licorice, maybe the occasional bowl of *kimchee* if I'm feeling frisky, and Korean.

If I could train myself to starve (or purge—beggars can't be choosy), I could be thin like Bex, dancing up against Jamal.

I need to escape this hallway with the view toward Jamal and Bex, but my legs feel locked in place while theirs move to the rhythm. He's got his hands on Bex's bony hips, fully exposed by her low-slung jeans that ride about a centimeter above her crotch. Very subtle. Bex's hands wrap around Jamal's neck as her hips make a futile white-girl two-step effort to sway in time to the music's beat. He's leaning down to her, smiling, inviting; it's almost like he's going to kiss her. Except she's a vanilla girl who's not supposed to be on his color palette of girl hues. He whispers in her ear. She laughs. I hate her even more.

Jamal kisses a lot of girls but never me. He doesn't see me as a girl. To him I'm just a Miles, the sidekick. He doesn't judge me, he accepts me warts and all—"warts" being the operative word.

Bex's pants ride so low, they look like they could fall

down. She's even skinnier now than when I saw her at the funeral.

I'm not even high yet, but still I hear Laura whispering in my ear: *She's too thin, even for Bex. Something's not right.*

Only something has to be right with it. Jamal can't take his eyes off Bex's body.

Bex is so lucky. Her grief metabolism must swing on the appetite loss side of the pendulum. Mine swings toward bingeing.

That does it. I should make the commitment. I'm going back on the starvation diet: one lean frozen entrée per day, and unlimited Red Bulls and Marlboros. It takes a lot of willpower, but the results are fantastic. I can get down two sizes in a matter of weeks. Too bad about how I'll gain four back when I go back to the regular binge cycle.

Floyd notices me as he steps down the stairs into the hallway. Strands of long, greasy, strawberry-blond hair fall over his chin covered in stubble. I suspect he shaves about as often as he shampoos. He wears a long and tattered granny cardigan sweater. With a tie belt. Disconcertingly, he appears to perk up at the sight of me—or to perk up as much as a guy whose eyelids are perpetually half closed can. "Hey, Miles." He tucks a strand of greasy hair behind his ear. "I've been hoping to see you. I wanted to tell you I'm really sorry about your sister—"

"She was my cousin."

"She was so pretty like you, I figured she had to be your sister."

I'd be more flattered if Jamal had heard Floyd's comment. Does he notice me here with Floyd? Would he care that somebody, maybe, is attracted to me?

It could happen. Not every man sees only size. Some sense depth.

"What's cooking tonight?" I ask Floyd.

"What's your pleasure?" My feet finally cooperate, called to action by the goodies that will be found by following Floyd to the kitchen. There, we sit down on stools and Floyd takes some plastic baggies from the worn-out pockets of his granny sweater and spreads them across the long, marble countertop.

"Nope," I say to the dope.

I shake my head at the coke. Gross.

The third bag, the pill bag, is the charm. "That'll do me."

How soon can I get there? How soon?

"Miles!" Jamal approaches my side, sweat glistening on his brow from the dancing, but no Bex in tow. "Could you go check on Bex? She took off suddenly for the bathroom. I'm worried something's wrong."

Floyd tells Jamal, "The house's rest room areas are not marked as being for either Girls or Boys. It's a unisex free-for-all stall situation here. It's okay to check on your girl yourself. Can't you see I'm sharing a moment with your lady?"

"But what if it's a girl thing?" Jamal asks him, and

suddenly he and Floyd are united on this front.

"Yeah, you'd better check on her," Floyd tells me.

I roll my eyes. "Whatever." I never say no to Jamal.

What a princess. I find her upstairs in the best bathroom in the house, in Floyd's parents' unused bedroom, the one room untouched by the evening's denizens. It's the bathroom with the bidet and the Jacuzzi and the sunroof and the enormous glass shower stall that seems bigger than my bedroom. I expect to find Bex with a proud finger down her throat at the gilded toilet, but instead she's sitting on it, her pants still on, leaning her head against the tile wall at her side.

Crying.

Bex wipes away her tears, tries to compose herself. She acts like nothing's wrong, like of course I would find her in the Buckingham Palace bathroom so we could have a proper chat. She says, "I saw that Floyd guy checking you out. I think he likes you. Do you like him?"

"He's just being friendly." Like I can't see through her act, trying to be nice to me to get to Jamal. "Why are you crying?"

Hungry?

"You really want to know?"

Not really, but why don't you tell me anyway.

I nod, move a couple inches closer to her. She could touch my hand or something if she needed comfort. I'm doing my part.

"It doesn't feel right," Bex says. "Being here tonight, without her." Now here's a strange and unfamiliar feeling not caused by a mind-altering substance: I agree with Bex.

But I say nothing.

She takes a deep breath, almost as if to calm herself, but her next words are anything but refined. "I HATE HER! HOW COULD SHE DO THIS TO US?"

I do want to speak now, to tell Bex that I understand, that I am shocked we could share any kind of mutual emotion, but she storms out of the bathroom before I open my mouth.

I hate Laura too. The hatred surges sudden and raw. Unexpected. Even when Laura and I went through stages when we weren't close, I never didn't love her, never didn't feel part of her.

She didn't fight hard enough. She deserted us.

Accu-Miles Storm Center Report, live on the scene: This intrepid reporter did not fail to come upstairs armed and ready. I can hold down the fort from this bathroom. Ride it out here while Bex returns to the eye of the storm downstairs. I take out the plastic pill baggie from my pocket and instinctively reach for two pills from the bag. Then I remember. I return Laura's to the bag, then remove the outer coating from the one for me. I can save Laura's for another day. A rainy-day promise for the future.

Ah, here it is. Finally. Yes.

It's sinking in as I sink down the wall. This is the rest of our lives, without her.

Burnout

AM I STILL HIGH?

Or did Floyd, who's given me a lift home after I passed out in his parents' bathroom at Crash Landing, really hold open his car door for me and then mumble something about whether I wanted to go see a movie with him sometime, or whatever? I have to be hallucinating, because no way did some guy not named Jamal ask me somewhere, or whatever.

If only I was hallucinating. But the smell of leaking transmission fluid from the trailer-slash-meal-truck parked on the street alerts me to the morning's reality: It's not Jim I need to dodge as I stumble back home. It's the biological entity known as my father.

Is it just me, or do other daughters have a dad who lives out of a creaky, smelly, dirty mobile home that doubles as what he lovingly refers to as a "roach coach," from which he sells sandwiches at construction sites to eke out a living?

Television perpetuates the lie that dads are reliable, loving creatures who earn stable livings and can be counted on to tackle home improvement projects—with disastrous and hilarious results, along with some doting advice snuck in to the kids. Who *gets* that dad? I certainly didn't. Mine can legitimately repair a roof, fix a dishwasher, or install drywall, but ask him what day is my birthday, when did I first walk, my first word, the name of any school I've attended, and he'll draw a blank. Don't ask him to kick in for child support. He's broke and proud of it. He wants for nothing beyond his mobile home and the hope that some skinny, perky blonde will turn letters on *Wheel of Fortune* until she literally keels over, dead but smiling.

Maybe I'm too hard on Buddy. He himself makes no pretense of having fatherly ambitions, so why should I hold him accountable as a daughter? This is a guy I've called "Buddy" my whole life, and not because it's his name, but because when I was a small child and he didn't understand the concept of how to address a "daughter," he would call me "Buddy" instead of my name; I just gave the nickname back to him, not understanding then the concept of a man who would answer to "Daddy." For Laura, such a man could exist, but even then I knew: not for me.

The neighbors typically complain every summer

about the monstrous vision of Buddy's mobile home sullying their historic thoroughfare of historic homes. There's plenty of room for Buddy's trailer in the parking area inside the gates of Jim's compound, where Jim's collection of vehicles are kept: his Volvo, two BMWs from paramours no longer *amour,* Laura's untouched hybrid graduation present, an ancient Rolls Royce that belonged to Jim's mother that he's never been able to part with. But the neighbors atypically can't turn to Jim for support on the roach coach issue; his civility does not extend to his civic duty where that trailer is concerned. Jim requests Buddy not to park there because the trailer leaks fluid not just on the parking area pavement, but also, more importantly, across the ancient cobblestones leading from the iron gate at the street to the parking lot behind the big house. Big *Architectural Digest* no-no.

I could care less about the opinions of the Georgetown community, but I'm with Jim on this one. I prefer that the dilapidated trailer be parked on the main street. I'd rather have my father out there than in here. Buddy loves that mobile home and won't stay in the carriage house except to use the kitchen or the shower when he parks here for summer visits. Works fine by me. It would work better for me if he didn't come *at all*, but I haven't negotiated that freedom yet.

I turn eighteen this August. I will no longer be obligated to tolerate Buddy's summer sabbaticals as my temporary chaperone-from-a-trailer-parked-on-the-street. So, happy ending: I will ultimately have something to give back to the community.

Buddy sits outside the carriage house in the beat-up, plastic foldout chair he reserves for "guests" in his mobile home as I approach my charity home. "You look like hell, kid." His gravel, country voice doesn't sound concerned so much as amused. I quickly take mental inventory of the appliances in the carriage house—what needs fixing? Better to put Buddy right on the case before he jumps ship. "Is there a boyfriend in the picture these days that I have to talk to about returning you home before ten in the morning?"

Now it's my turn to laugh. A boyfriend returning me home after a wild night out? Right. That's not a problem heavy girls generally need to worry about. Heart disease and diabetes—maybe. Getting some—not really.

I turn to face Buddy. I don't know how I sprung from his DNA. We look nothing alike. He's tall and wiry where I am short and chubby. My hair may be black and curly like his, but that's hair dye on my part, and humidity on D.C.'s part. And I would never cover my head with a red bandanna or allow my death-pallor skin to acquire trucker tan on my arms and neck.

Buddy looks me up and down, taking inventory of me. I'm another year older, and fuller—he must notice that. But his observation is: "You're burnt out, kid."

Takes one to know one. At least he's not so phoney as to fake concern. He has no problem looking irritated, however. Chaperoning a daughter who's a burnout—just one more thing he'll have to deal with in his hardship life responsible to no one but himself, living out of a trailer and selling cheese sandwiches to connoisseurs too desperate to find sustenance farther than where Buddy has shown up for the day—right in their face.

I kick aside the doormat and point to the key on the ground. He could have let himself in. He forgets about that key every year. All those years of my childhood he lost to drugs and alcoholism cost him key brain memory cells. That substance scenario won't happen to me. My DNA code was shared with Laura. We're all or nothing.

I step inside the house. I want my bed and for Buddy not to be here. "Nice to see you too, Miles," he calls out from behind me.

The sarcasm. Got that from him.

He follows me inside. "I left you a message telling you I was arriving this morning."

"Oh." I pop open a Coke from the fridge.

"Do you even listen to your messages?"

"No."

I go into the hall closet and find some clean towels, hand them to him, and proceed to my bedroom. I am about to close the bedroom door, but he's standing right there, holding his hand out to prevent the door closing.

"Laura," he says.

I say nothing. Can't even offer "I'm fine."

He offers: "It's, like, totally weird to be here now and know she's not going to come through the door at any moment looking for you. Do you, like, want to talk about it?"

The question sounds, like, rehearsed.

He gets plenty of emoting at his AA meetings. Doesn't need it from me.

"No." *Please, let me shut this door in your face. And tell your sponsor not to advise you to pretend to console me just to make YOU feel better.*

Yet I leave the door open, opening him up to continue, "Mel didn't tell me until after the funeral was already over. I'm sorry. I would have been there."

Even in death Laura overshadows me. Buddy's missed all the important events in my life so far—yet he would have wanted to come to Laura's funeral.

If I wasn't burnt-out right now, I would lose it. The aftermellow allows me simply to remain silent.

"Help me out here, kid? Don't you have anything to say to your old man?"

Last summer he gave me twenty bucks to go to an Al-Anon meeting while he went to one of his AA meetings. I repeat back to him an AA adage from a poster I saw on the wall there: "Don't speak unless you can improve on silence."

I close my bedroom door.

Escape Hatch

THE INFORMATION CONSPIRACY WILL BE TELEVISED. LOCATE your escape hatch.

Round-the-clock "news" feeds (D.C.-area commuter traffic update immediately followed by Middle East bombing followed by celebrity divorce update then back to hellfire terror images) flash from television monitors everywhere—at the grocery store checkout line, the post office, train stations, cafés. No innocent bystander shall be left wanting for information.

I prefer to be uninformed. Perhaps I can't escape the fact of the "news" force-feed, but I can, simply, close my eyes. If I visualize a chocolate cupcake and settling into a hydro and a book at bedtime, I can block out the backup on the inner loop of the Beltway, or the international faces of anguish that the "news" blurbheads, selling Hondas in between the images of hopelessness and horror, must want to numb me to in their relentless quest to inform inform inform me.

Please. Be quiet.

Despite the bombardment of information coming from all sides, whether you want the information or not, there's still so much that can effectively be blocked out. Sunblock to protect the skin. Antihistamine to block the itchies. A computer keystroke to block an online pervert. Unfortunately I went to bed in too much of a haze to turn on the white noise machine I keep in my nightstand specifically for summertime—to block out cicada noise, and the grating sound of Buddy's voice and his strangely high-pitched, girly laugh.

I hear him through my bedroom window. He's out in the garden with Jim, probably sitting in my seat. He'd better not be smoking my cigarettes. I'm on a budget.

The setting sun beams through the window shades as I wake to the conversation of the Odd Couple in the garden. They're talking about sandwiches.

Jim: "This is surprisingly tasty for a cheese sandwich."

Buddy: "It's brie, man. Gotta go with brie. And fresh bread. Always. Fresh basil, too, if you can score it. Heh-heh." He cackles. I shudder.

Is there a pill to keep me asleep through the rest of the summer?

Alas, hunger prevails. It always does with me.

"Good evening, Miles," Jim says when I find my way out to them at the garden patio table. He's so formal, with a proper linen napkin on his lap, waiting to address me until he's completely swallowed that tasty brie.

"Seven o'clock in the evening always your wake time, Miles?" From Mr. Suave, napkinless, mouth still full. The gourmand added ketchup to his sandwich.

"She's a night crawler, like me," Jim tells Buddy.

"I set out a sandwich for you," Buddy says. The sandwich is wrapped in wax paper, cut down the middle, and awaiting me on a dinner plate.

"I'm lactose intolerant." I pour the Coke I've brought out to the garden into a glass of ice and reach for Buddy's bag of potato chips.

"Since when?" Buddy asks. He stares too intently into my eyes. It's weird. "Mel shoulda told me. That's important."

Am I supposed to care that my father, who went three years when I was a child without a single phone call, letter, or visit to me, on account of being too wasted to remember the fact of his seedage left behind in Georgetown, has all of a sudden decided to care? Because caring—it's really not an emotion I can conjure that easily. Either I block it or I don't.

"Miles isn't lactose intolerant," Jim tells Buddy. I detect a slight twinkle in his eye as he glances in my direction. "She's teasing you."

"Oh." Buddy places his feet up on the glass table. A single look from Jim and he places them back on the ground.

I light a cigarette. "You're not of legal age to buy cigarettes. Where are you getting these?" Buddy again.

Fake ID. Heard of it? He turns to Jim. "You let her smoke here?"

Jim lights his own cigarette. "She's got a mind of her own, and she understands the health risks. This has been a difficult time for us both. I'm inclined to think we're allowed this vice—at least right now."

Just let us survive the summer without her. If we can do that, we'll figure out the rest later. Deal with the cancer part when it happens.

"I gave up smoking last winter," Buddy says. "'Lord, I ain't what I oughta be, I ain't what I am going to be, but Lord, oh Lord, I thank you that I ain't what I used to be.'"

AA again. Character choosing to play caricature again.

Jim responds in AA-speak: "'You don't need to "find God." He isn't lost.'"

"What?" asks Buddy.

I stifle a giggle.

"Are we paranoid?" I direct the question to Jim.

"How so?"

How quickly Buddy is blocked out, and it's just me and Jim again, smoking and talking. Just like old times, just like yesterday. "I mean, is the rest of the world out to get us? Why do they hate us so much?"

I need to understand hate before I can understand how to live in the world Laura opted out of. Buddy's presence alone is enough indication to make me understand: I can only block out so much. The strategy isn't foolproof.

"That's a big question," Jim says.

"Does the rest of the world figure that the root of all evil emanates out of Washington alone, or is Washington just the decoy to pin all the blame on?" There's a difference between "Washington" and "D.C.", and that difference is those who come here to rape and pillage domestic and foreign policy, and those who are born and bred here, who care about the actual city, the non-federal government blocks. "We live here trapped in ground zero for all the world's antagonism, yet our own citizens in the nation's capital, who reside in the apex of the land of supposed freedom, actually have no real rights to influence our country's agenda. We just have to live with the hate. You're a D.C. native, Jim. You always say it's a completely different city now than the one you grew up in. More sophisticated, but more sterile, less respected—and totally paranoid. How did this happen to D.C.?"

"Used to be a cow town," Buddy chimes in.

We ignore him.

"What changed?" I ask Jim.

Jim responds, "You can start with our Cold War paranoia, I guess. Any Soviet bloc country that built an embassy here was sure to be plotting nuclear war against us, right in our own backyard. But the anxiety and intrigue of that time also came with the relative comfort that we were indeed just paranoid. Now the paranoia is for real reasons." Jim's index finger points upward, to a plane flying low overhead.

I find it fascinating that post-World War II suburban

Americans used to build bunkers in their backyards, they were so sure The Bomb was going to drop on them. Who'd want to come out of such an escape hatch, survive the aftermath of an apocalypse? Better to just die in the maelstrom. Don't live to see the cookie-cutter dream world destructed.

I ask Jim, "What was it like to live in D.C. when it was a place that was admired instead of loathed? Was it so Camelot-enchanted that its own citizens, the real ones, not the transients, didn't notice they were living in a state of taxation without representation?"

"Miles, are you actually expressing civic pride and outrage—or at least interest? I'll be sure to phone Dr. Turner. She's got some D.C. committee work she needs help on this summer."

How nice. Jim wants to save me, like he wants to save everybody.

It was his own daughter who needed saving, not me.

"You sure have a lot to say for a girl who just woke up, Miles." Buddy. *Again.*

I sure have a lot to say for a girl whose best friend didn't call her once today to see if she made it home okay from the party he ditched her at last night so he could hit on an anorexic bimbo who's not even *from* D.C., legitimately.

Jim says, "I'm going to go call Dr. Turner right now, in fact. Good evening, folks." He gets up to leave. The amazing part is, I gave him the escape hatch from Buddy without realizing it. *You're welcome, Jim. You owe me.*

"You seem pretty smart, kid," Buddy says to me once Jim is gone. "Tell me something about yourself."

"Like what?"

"I don't know. What do you want to be?"

"That's a big question." In another time, I would have wanted to be a writer who traveled the world in search of adventure, and torrid love affairs. But the world feels closed off to me now, blocked, based on the sins of past presidents. And size two is the new size six. I'm ten sizes up, on a good day, from the old new size.

"Here's a bigger one," Buddy says. There had better not be another AA saying coming. "Your pupils are dilated and your walk is all wrong." Mel never noticed. "You want to tell me why you're doing pharms?"

Could we go back to what I want to be?

I don't care enough to lie. "To feel something other than what I feel now."

"Which is what?"

Despair.

I also don't care enough to let Buddy in further. "Nothing. I'm fine."

When I'm high, I don't have to *try* to block out anything, or anyone. When I'm high, I'm not fat, and Jamal is all mine, and the world is safe and understandable. No escape hatch necessary—I'm already living inside it. I'm allowed the suspension of disbelief.

"You're not fine. And I joined the union just so you could have health insurance, so why don't you see a shrink or something? You know what that health insurance costs me? Might as well use it." He says this as though I should feel grateful for this luxury that Mel insisted he bestow upon me, in lieu of monetary support to us, ever. Ketchup drips from Buddy's sandwich on to his tattered white T-shirt. "I remember what it was like at your age, feeling like it's your right to experiment. But do you want to hear about the friends I had who didn't live to tell? C'mon, Miles. You're smarter than that. Don't be a loser like your old man. Look what it'll get ya."

Honeysuckle Sweet

⚜

ONCE UPON A TIME, TWO SISTER–COUSINS IN A TREE HOUSE played a game called Good Housekeeping.

When they were thirteen-going-on-fourteen, in a soot-covered, untended bookshelf at their favorite old neighborhood bookstore, they had discovered what would become their reading Bible that summer: *The Good Housekeeping Cook Book,* 1942 edition. The D.C. summer days were so hot that the cobblestone pavement in their garden appeared to roll, the air felt still, the trees wilted in exhaustion. At twilight, when the temperature became bearable, the two girls took refuge away from the castle's air conditioning to slip inside their shaded fortress tree house, where they read aloud passages from their new archeological discovery.

AFTERNOON TEA FOR A FEW: Half an hour to get it, and clear it away, if you're busy. An hour or longer, if you're having a few friends in. But the very act of appearing serene, makes you feel that way. And the hot tea with a dainty accompaniment or two, helps to turn your mind to happy repose.

They drank iced tea with fresh mint from the garden and imagined what a "happy repose" could possibly be. They had discovered cigarettes but not yet the fresh herbs and other bloodstream enhancements that could truly make them feel serene. One of them had kissed a boy already. One of them would wait much, much longer, possibly forever.

They knew they would grow old together, best friends always—but more, because they were blood. They acted out Good Housekeeping future sister-lives that included lavish weddings, palatial homes, beautiful children, and always—*always*—a properly-set table, using the good linens, real dinner napkins, a floral centerpiece, candles, and the silver grudgingly passed down from a domineering mother-in-law.

A formal dinner party calls for damask in either linen or a very fine rayon, with a table pad beneath it for protection, or an allover lace or embroidered cloth laid on the bare table. In laying such cloths have the center fold running down the exact center of the table. The cloth should overhang about 8"-10".

They kept a ruler in the tree house, and discussed anatomical parts that could be wedged within that 8"-10" overhang. By the end of their Good Housekeeping summer, one of them had touched, through a pair of jeans, an upper thigh near to the very anatomy that hung between the legs of a boy at summer camp. The other had not, but she could rely on books and/or her better half for anecdotal evidence.

OVERWEIGHT AT THE TEEN AGE: In many families there is a boy or girl who is definitely overweight. It is true that some extra pounds through adolescence are not harmful and they are often lost naturally as the child matures. But to be excessively overweight presents a real problem both to the child and the parents. There is often ridicule from companions which causes hurt feelings and a withdrawal from companions, resulting in a hesitancy about entering into active sports, so that the child does not get the proper exercise as well as the desirable association with other children. There may even be some dulling mentally, though often the reverse is true because the child may turn to intensive reading and study to fill his time to compensate for the lack of companionship and other outlets.

Of the two girls, the wider, duller half was mentally astute enough to invent a Good Housekeeping product for their game, an air freshener she branded "Honeysuckle Sweet." The two girls sprayed imaginary Honeysuckle Sweet throughout the tree house as they acted out commercials advertising the product. In their favorite commercial, a happily married gay couple's union was threatened by unfortunate, embarrassing incidents of bathroom odor; lucky for this wholesome couple to have Honeysuckle Sweet to mist through the awkwardness. The two girls didn't understand why these commercials weren't on television already. The families they understood were never represented unless they themselves created commercials portraying them.

The summer the left behind girl was seventeen-going-on-eighteen, her back-up best friend represents in the tree house at twilight. He wants to talk about the backup best friend to the girl who was now gone.

"I think this is it," he says. "*The* girl. The one to change my life. Bex."

The left behind girl remembers an evening not many months earlier, when she and her sister-cousin were strung out on weed, mellow and silly. The lighthearted, lightweight girl had just chosen to attend Georgetown University the following year. The weighty other girl was weighing dropping out of high school entirely. As they passed a joint, the weighty girl made up a story imagining the future wedding of the college-bound girl: After graduating Georgetown with a degree in foreign affairs, beloved sister-girl would marry her high school sweetheart, he who was truthfully only partially beloved and this girl would marry him mostly because she was used to him—but she could conduct foreign affairs secretly to keep her entertained if she so desired. The royal bride would break with tradition and wear a gown made of table linens, damask or a very fine rayon, but never allover lace (tacky). The chapel would be lined with Honeysuckle Sweet bottles rather than floral arrangements. The bottles would be situated exactly 8"-10" apart. After the ceremony, guests would spray air freshener rather than throw rice at the mostly happy couple. The wedding cake would be tiered in fresh honeysuckle. The bride and groom would toast their union with honeysuckle wine.

It was a good story and a fabulous wedding, and the two girls in the tree house giggled through the sweet haze of their happy repose. Then the prospective story bride, coughing between hits, announced that she would not live to see the day of her own wedding. At the time, the other girl—who would have worn the honeysuckle-hued maid of honor dress but not sleeveless; that would be tacky on a plump girl—thought this rejection simply meant the story bride would chose a different groom. Or a better dress. That was all. The storyteller girl didn't understand: The princess bride already knew she would be cutting off her own future, in real life. She was trying to prepare her lady-in-weighting.

"You can't be serious," the left-behind girl says to the boy in the twilight tree house. After. "You've only known her a couple weeks. You met her at a funeral."

The left-behind girl thinks, *If I were thin, could I have been her? The girl?*

She has a physical feeling when this boy is near her; she can feel him in every ounce of her flesh, in every single beat of her heart. She wonders if she is lying to herself and to him by acting like she wants nothing more from him than friendship. Could that lie kill their friendship?

But she's had enough of death for now. She's not ready to let him go, too. Not yet.

"I don't want to go to Morehouse, Miles. That's my parents' path for me. *Their* dream, not mine. Bex is going to Columbia in the fall. I might want to follow her to New York. *My* dream is to become an actor. New York's a place to do that."

His cocoa face is cast in the tree house window's tangerine sunset light as he speaks. He is a vision of perfection, completely unaware as he talks that the girl in whom he is confiding literally wants to die hearing him profess his powerful new feelings for a skinny vanilla girl called Bex.

The girl called Miles wishes she could tell this Jamal boy all that she loves about him. His daring. His talent. His crooked smile with the two crooked bottom teeth that only brighten his handsome dark face. His kindness, his loyalty, the smell of him, his honeysuckle sweetness. He has never accepted her for anything less than who she is. He seeks out and enjoys her company where so few others will dare. He confides in her, considers her to be his dearest friend of the heart and soul.

Her heart and soul share that feeling of friendship, but also feel . . . attraction.

She understands: She doesn't love this boy. She is *in* love with this boy. Previously she only understood the distinction between "love" and "in love" from reading about it in books. This feels real. Shame.

If she could only tell him the sum total of all she loves in him, he'd know she wasn't some ignorant kid who couldn't possibly understand or could experience love; he'd see that she knows it and she hurts for it.

"Bex is hurting," this boy tells the left-behind girl

who is *in* love with him. "She wants to talk to you about Laura. But she thinks you don't like her."

It's not the loving that hurts this girl; it's the understanding of it for what it is, that it will never be returned in the same way, that threaten to destroy her. But to unload the words—"I love you"—on an innocent party who didn't ask for it, to reach across the dark space and touch him—it's like the world she knows could end if she dared speak these words, dared make such a move.

She wonders if her heart could simply stop beating for being so unwanted in return.

She doesn't want the boy causing the distinction between "love" and "in love" to see her cry, so she nods her assent; she'll try to like Bex. She asks this boy to fetch her an iced tea with fresh mint from the garden. He loves her without the "in"; he will go.

She wishes the went-away girl was here now to play their old game, to help her invent a better ending.

Power to the People

DR. TURNER HAS HER SCHOOLHOUSE, HER CAUSES, HER willful determination. She's so Jo in *Little Men*.

Sojourner Truth Charter Academy, her brainchild, my soon-to-not-be high school, is located in a converted waterfront warehouse at the river's edge of Georgetown. Some rich folk donate their money and real estate to fund hospitals and orphanages. Jim chooses to allocate his resources to his friends and their shared cause to better the D.C. public school system—specifically, by establishing charter schools that offer alternative education to all the crap that hasn't been working in the past.

I go along with Dr. Turner because the whole idea of her—Supermom and superprincipled high school principal along with super D.C. advocate, someone who cares so much—is so quaint as to possibly be inspiring.

In my fantasy future life, I could have grown up to become Dr. Turner's super daughter-in-law: helping her out with charity events, lending a confidant's ear when her perfect daughter Niecy rebels and dates the wrong guy (of course, I'd play the same angle with Niecy, railing against her mom to me in private sessions with her trusted sister-in-law), fixing a nutritionally-balanced but delicious dinner for Jamal when he comes home from work at night. Dr. Turner could count on me to Do the Right Thing.

In real time, I sit in my niche spot since kindergarten—the principal's office. Only we're not discussing my behavioral problems. Not yet, at least. Niecy and I are in Dr. Turner's office, going through boxes and boxes of voter registration records, highlighting names and addresses for a future phone drive that will solicit funds and signatures for a D.C. statehood petition. Jim volunteered me to the cause, and I stepped up by not volunteering to unvolunteer me. It might not be so terrible to want to impress the big guy in the big house, even in some small way—besides sharing my smokes with him.

Anything to make this dreadful summer go by faster. Fill her void.

"That's some trailer your daddy's got parked on Jim's street," Niecy teases. "What, did he win that thing off some game show—twenty years ago?" She hums along to the R&B song playing on the radio. I don't sing along with her. "You're so sensitive, Miles. Don't make that face at me, I didn't mean it in a bad way. I like your daddy's trailer. Brings some character to the neighborhood. And he makes good sandwiches, yeah." Niecy opens the wax paper on the smoked gouda baguette Buddy delivered earlier this morning.

"Doubt Buddy will be around for long," I assure her.

"Not according to Mama." A fifteen-year-old girl can't help but share the gossip; it's basic biological instinct to her. Niecy leans in toward me and whispers, "Jim went ape-crazy when your mama left for London so soon after Laura passed. There was some kind of battle that went on behind the scenes. I heard Mama talking to Jim about it on the phone. I guess Mel told Jim you were old enough to be on your own now, didn't need or want anybody around anymore anyway, but Jim told Mel, 'Not true!' and said, either you have a parent at the house, or Mel needed to take you to London with her. So get used to those sandwiches, girl."

It goes without saying that the terms of Mel and Jim's secret negotiations would have come down to whether or not I would remain having a home at all at the carriage house. I don't know how people manage who have no home. Where would I go.

I still don't say anything back to Niecy. "Want me to braid your hair again?" she asks. "You look so nice when that nappy-wild hair is braided and people can actually see your face. You know how pretty you are, right, Miles?"

Thank you for the lie, truly pretty girl. But I guess I wasn't pretty enough.

"So Jamal and Bex, huh?" I say. I haven't seen him in

a week, since Bex completed her takeover of him.

"Won't last," Niecy assures me. She waves her hand, dismissive. "They're spirits in the dark, getting through a rough time together, is all. It'll fade. Like magic."

It feels almost supernatural to be in a school in the summertime, as if surely gremlins and goblins should taunt us from the ceiling: *Out, damn people! Summertime, and the living is queasy. This is OUR playhouse this time of year. Don't you know the rules?*

The rules were supposed to be that Jamal doesn't date white girls, and daughters of Congressmen Same Old White Men could never express an interest in the son of D.C.'s upper-class black elite.

Niecy bites into her sandwich, then announces, "Mama oughta add these sandwiches to the cafeteria menu at this school. They're awesome. Want a piece of mine?"

I'm already full from the half bag of cookies I snarfed down in the bathroom, in private. I shake my head. I don't want a sandwich. I want sweetness. I want to be daring, like her brother. I want to be pretty, like Niecy, and a tell-all, too. I tell her, "I'm probably not coming back to school this fall."

"Shut up. Where are you going?"

"Dropping out. I don't belong in school." It's not like I know what I'll do when I drop out. Probably I'll try to get a full-time job or something. I'll figure out it after I sign the papers. I don't think Jim expects me to move out once I turn of legal age. But I'm not sure. The only thing I am sure of is that I'm too scared to ask him directly.

Niecy won't need to resist the urge to tattle on me. Her mother stands in the doorway, and she's heard all. Dr. Turner addresses Niecy with a simple, "You are excused, baby."

Niecy's look to me says, *You're on your own, girl.* She grabs her sandwich, deposits a kiss on Mama's cheek, and swiftly leaves the principal's office.

Dr. Turner sits down in her chair at her desk, opposite me.

"You'll drop out of school over my dead body, Miles."

Speaking of dead bodies, I glance at the wall behind Dr. Turner's head. It's lined with so many award plaques and degrees, it would be natural to assume someone so lauded must secretly be a murderer or at least an embezzler who knows where the bodies are buried.

"Miles? Do you have something to say for yourself? Because in case you didn't hear me properly—"

"She's out to get me."

"Who?"

"Mrs. Campbell." I've done my best not to think about her since school let out, since Laura, but being back in this school now, I can't help but not. Remember how much I hate her.

Mrs. Campbell, head demon terrorizing this schoolhouse, became the creative writing as well as literature teacher last winter when the creative writing teacher took maternity leave. The first creative writing teacher gave me an A-, said I had a unique way of looking at the world through words. Mrs. Campbell gave me a C+. According to Mrs. Campbell, not only do I know nothing about great books, but there are also rules I should be obeying when constructing my own fiction—that is, *rules for stories that are supposed to be made up.* Also, I have no ability to tell a linear story (I don't even know what a linear story is so why would I want to write one?), and I'm derivative. And use run-on sentences.

"She's a fine teacher," Dr. Turner says. It's Dr. Turner's job to defend her teachers; I understand that. In their defense, most of the teachers at this school are pretty decent. There's just that one.

I give Dr. Turner her daughter's you've-got-to-be-kidding-me face in response.

What I like about Dr. Turner is I trust her not to lie to me. And she doesn't now: "Maybe Mrs. Campbell isn't a match for every student." Pause. "Her students test well." Pause. "She's not out to get you. She wants to uphold you to the highest standards, get the best work out of you."

I can read through Dr. Turner's not-lies: *This school's budget can't afford better.*

"What if Mrs. Campbell's standards aren't my standards?" I ask. "What if she's so hung up on rules and grammar that she can't recognize an original thought? Wasn't this school founded to foster creativity and independent thinking instead of obsessing over the forbidden run-on sentence?"

What if Mrs. Campbell is just one of those mean and bitter high school teachers that like their own opinions more than they like teenage students—whom they don't really seem to like at all, by the way?

Dr. Turner pulls out my file from a pile on her desk. It's a thick file. The problem students' case reports always are.

Dr. Turner says, "According to Mrs. Campbell's notes on your report card, you are a strong writer with an intelligent mind, but you need discipline. That seems like a fair criticism to me. What's the problem?"

"My own teacher states that I cannot achieve my only dream and yet she is supposed to be teaching me how to do it."

"She never said you couldn't pursue your dream."

"Not in those words, maybe. But she implied it."

"Miles." Dr. Turner smiles at Miles.

"What?" I don't get what I said to earn Dr. Turner's heartwarming expression. Mrs. Campbell and I are never going to share that uplifting, redemptive student–teacher bond found only in movies.

"You have a dream. Admit it."

I won't.

"I don't see the point in me continuing on with high school after I'm already eighteen." When Jamal has moved on without me.

"So your future ability to be gainfully employed and possibly pursue higher education means nothing to you?"

"Right."

"I don't believe you. Now here's a true challenge to you: *I* believe in you. So what's it going to take?"

"For what?"

"To make you give up on this nonsense idea of dropping out."

I didn't believe I could be talked out of it before now. I didn't believe anybody besides Laura could believe in me. "I want a different creative writing teacher."

"Can't do it. We're a small charter school, Miles. The only other qualified creative writing instructor I have teaches lower school."

I take the thick pile of voter registration records in my hands and slap them down onto Dr. Turner's desk with exaggerated, dramatic, derivative movie effect. "Then I want the ability to protest. When Mrs. Campbell says I can't write a story that supposedly should have infinite possibilities, or that I misread a book that's completely open to subjective debate, then I want to petition for a second opinion on my grade. Because that lady doesn't know what she's talking about."

Dr. Turner raises her fist. "Done. Power to the people."

Hey, Mrs. Campbell: Guess where to find me. I'll be the student returning to your classroom just to spite you.

I didn't know I had it in me. Caring, about; Skool.

Snow Day

THE NOON DAY BURNS BRUTALLY HOT AND HUMID. I aspire to perspire the afternoon away in the dark, solitary caverns of the bookstore's tall, dusty bookcases. I'll turn off the cranky window A/C that spits dust and lukewarm rather than chill air. I'll sit near the window that begs for a breeze to come through it. Bake the day inside a book.

My day's game plan is obstructed by the vision of Team Jamal & Bex standing in front of the bookstore as I approach it.

Even my safe havens are no longer safe. Bookstore = sacred spot. Why'd he have to bring *her* here?

They're probably waiting for me with some lame idea to kidnap me on an adventure.

Pass.

Go, team. GO!

They're so tight in each other they don't notice me walking down the cobblestoned street toward them.

They're not making out as one could assume their teenage idle time hormones would dictate. It's worse. It's the easy familiarity of his arm around her shoulder, her head nestled inside his neck, that's so unsettling. When I see Jamal lean into her, I think, *Please don't let me have to see you kiss her mouth.* But he smiles at Bex rather than kiss her, then tucks a stray strand of her hair behind her ear, and tenderly, so tenderly, rubs his index finger along her earlobe.

That's the move that kills me.

The sweet possessiveness of it.

His hand that's many times held mine but never once delicately traced a random spot on my flesh.

Jealousy hot flashes through my body, a thunderbolt crashing through. It makes me want to run over to Bex and smash her to pieces. Set something afire.

Crimes of passion: suddenly understood.

If I proceed in their direction, I'm doubting I can keep it together. Hanging out with them would be a form of torture.

So I turn around before they notice me. So much for a work day.

I'll pretend it's a snow day. One on which I don't commit first degree murder.

I'm not so keen on sharing. Must be an only child problem. Last summer I had exclusive access to Jamal's free time.

I don't want a death sentence for my crime of wanting what can never be mine. I can commune with the dead instead.

I run past Rock Creek and take amnesty at another of my Georgetown sacred spots, Oak Hill Cemetery, the centuries-old garden park historical cemetery, home to the tombstones and mausoleums of the crème de la crème of Washington history, with grave surnames like Renwick, Corcoran, Van Ness, the namesakes of so many D.C. streets, buildings, and neighborhoods. Inside a den of tall trees and grounds springing azaleas, daffodils and apple blossoms, the dead here can at least brag, *Hey now, we got the best view.*

I picked a good day to idle with ghosts. What rational living person would want to bake here in the middle of D.C. summer? The cemetery grounds are mostly empty save for a few stray tourists with cameras and wilting hair. Northern Europeans are so dear but uninformed about weather patterns in American cities built on swamps.

I sit on the wrought-iron bench on the path outside the gothic cemetery chapel. Laura and I used to bring our sleds here on snow days. When we rested on this bench, inspecting the snow-covered terrain under the stark, leaveless oak trees, as the setting winter sun tinted light through the oranges and yellows of the chapel's stained-glass windows, we were pretty sure we'd stumbled on the path to Heaven. Looking now at the ancient stone chapel, the stained-glass windows almost swallowed by the surrounding lush greens of grass and trees, I have to mad respect the majesty "God" inspires others to build for Him. Although I fervently believe in the scientific *fact* that the universe was created billions of years ago, and no way did He have anything to do with it, the Book of Cool Fiction, I mean Genesis, notwithstanding, I will concede that the art sprung from the passion over the centuries is mad good.

"Don't tell me. You're asking, What would Jesus do?" The voice belongs to Niecy, who is standing on the path by the bench, her arms crossed over her chest, glaring at me, and sweating. "'Cuz I'm gonna tell you what He'd say. He'd say, 'Milcs, in case you haven't noticed, it's ninety-six degrees out here, not a cloud in the sky, and there's been such an invention called AIR-CONDITIONING to help out with this kind of situation.'"

"Were you sent to fetch me?" In order for spots to be sacred, there can only be a few of them. This makes it difficult to survive a You Can't Find Me expedition.

"Jamal said I might find you here."

"Why are you looking for me?"

"Maybe I'm not looking for you. Maybe I'm just trying to look out *for* you."

"*For* what?"

I can only be grateful she doesn't answer the question's challenge.

She sits down on the bench next to me. "Tell me a story. Make this hot day go away."

In the basement at Niecy and Jamal's house, there's an ancient PacMan video game that came along with the house when the family bought it. They never discarded the relic, and it has provided me endless hours of entertainment in the basement corner while Niecy and Jamal played sophisticated video games on the big screen TV nearby. It's the stupidest game, really. A "Pac-Man" mouth gobbles up dots as it proceeds through simple levels of not-challenge. It's stupid . . . but completely mesmerizing. I think the sadness that chips away inside me is like that Pac-Man game. It progressively gobbles away at my soul, a physical pain that no one can see, a prism that's virtually a prison. Clutching onto that sadness is like wielding a weapon; it's what Laura did, only she didn't wear it on a fat body the way I do. I think about her pain all the time lately. I imagine how much worse hers must have been than mine for it to have gripped her so badly, gotten so big and tortuous, that it finally gobbled her whole. She couldn't defeat it.

I don't know if I can either. But I can try. Not bolting away from Niecy is a step. Disenfranchisement.

"Once upon a time, there was a princess," I tell Niecy.

"Can she be a Nubian one? I get sick of all those Snow *White* characters."

"Surely. She's a chocolate princess named Snow."

"A black girl named 'Snow,' huh? I like it."

"Well, she's not really human. She's made of chocolate. She'll melt in the heat. It's like her Kryptonite. She needs to stay in cold climates to survive."

"How comes princesses always have some huge flaw that can cause their downfall?"

"I don't know. Plot?"

"Right, that."

"So this chocolate princess. Her knight in shining armor is the Easter Bunny."

"Naturally."

"But the Easter Bunny. He's sort of ambisexual. Questioning. And he's partial to the month of April. The climate variable is risky for his princess. Conflict."

"How's Snow going to deal?"

"She won't compromise. Snow tells E.B. he can have her only if he'll agree to hop around at acceptably cold latitudes. Plus, he's got to be a one-Snow bunny-man. She's not going to have a mate who's cheating on the side with, like, some St. Patrick's Day leprechaun, or any hussy tooth fairy. Sadly, E.B. does not get on board. He loves Snow, but he's not ready to commit, to make these sacrifices for her."

"Shame. His loss."

"I agree. So after losing the bunny-man she'd thought was her true love, Snow needs a fresh start. She moves to Canada. The really tippy-top part that's like glacial. She's gonna be alone and sad there, frigid but intact. But gradually, her heart starts to thaw, tho' her form remains choco-solid. She needs company. And since she's prac- tically in the North Pole and gets bored being alone, she seeks out Santa Claus. They hit it off, become buds. But Snow has to be kind of sneaky 'bout her friendship with Santa; Mrs. Claus is totally jealous of Snow's radiant chocolate beauty. It's hard, because everyone assumes Snow and Santa Claus are having an affair, but they're not at all. Their relationship is pure and based on mutual respect and understanding. The truth is never as interesting as what people whisper about them. But Snow and Santa Claus pay the gossip no mind. They form a strategic alliance and end up drafting an anti-global warming treatise that gets proposed at the United Nations."

"Good for them! But too bad about Snow and Santa. I'd like to know what happens when Santa gets his freak on."

"That's the sequel. When Mrs. Claus writes her tell-all memoir: *Claus-ette Effect: How a Chocolate Princess Stole My Man and All Because the Easter Bunny Wouldn't Put Out.*"

What's funny about our shared laughter is not the joke, but that the physical feeling of the laugh seems to ease off the bellyache of sad that's otherwise filling out my body.

And, the shared part.

Miles-napped

"DO YOU THINK SHE'S AT PEACE?"

This seems a strange question to ask a person over the sinks at a rest stop along the New Jersey Turnpike. Yet it also seems to be the only place where Bex and I connect: the bathroom.

I shake the water from my hands. Jamal has shaken me off for Bex, I sincerely probably hate her guts, but I have to respect Bex's good taste in people. "I wish that for Laura," I say, unsure. I can't decide whether I believe in an afterlife. I can't decide why anyone would *want* an afterlife. What's so great about living? "I want the comfort of believing Laura is happy wherever she is now, but wasn't her leaving us the way she did a statement that she didn't want to go on at all, in any way?" I have to respect the means to the end, too, even if the means mean Laura's soul is as dead as her body. She'd want no piece of peace.

"I have to believe you're wrong," Bex says. "That's

what comforts me when I wake up in the middle of the night from nightmares about what she did. I have to believe she's been forgiven up above, that—"

"Forgiven by God?"

"Yes, by God."

Good lord, how naive. I'm glad I was raised not to believe in any faith. Thanks for the atheism, checked-out parents!

"Does it give *you* peace to think she was forgiven by God?" I ask Bex.

"Yes. It does."

"Then you're not really worried about *Laura's* peace, are you? You're worried about your own."

Bex shakes the water from her hands—directly into my face. "You make it very difficult to like you."

I follow her out of the bathroom and into the parking lot. I don't protest her statement. I respect her for the acknowledgment. She *gets* me. There may be hope for us to be friends after all.

We climb into the backseat of the BMW in the parking lot. The car belongs to Laura's ex, Jason. He and Jamal sit in the front seat, a not very subtle attempt to give Bex and I "girl bonding" time on the drive up to New York City. I've chosen to sleep through the car ride instead. I'm no bond girl.

I wasn't given a choice about making this trip. Jamal awoke me at four in the morning by throwing pebbles at my bedroom window. Usually the pebble-throwing means he wants to wake me for a middle-of-the-night trip to IHOP, so I hopped right out of bed and jumped into the waiting car without questions. It was already moving by the time I realized both Jason and Bex were also in it, and the car was already leaving the District before I realized we were headed toward I-95 and not toward IHOP.

"What the . . . ?" I grumbled.

I need to stop choosing based on my stomach and my heart. I wish I could learn to turn those off.

"We've Miles-napped you," Jamal stated. "We're taking you on an adventure. Four hours up and away to the city that doesn't sleep."

"But . . . ," I started to protest.

"Don't worry, we cleared it with your dad first," Bex said.

"I *wasn't* worried," I snapped. Like I needed Buddy's permission to go somewhere I didn't even want to go to. I pretended to fall back asleep until I actually did.

Back on the road after the pit stop, we're soon driving through a section of New Jersey highway that's surrounded by power plants and swamps, and smells of raw sewage. The view from the car window looks like the cover art on an apocalyptic, hell dimension sci-fi novel.

"This is the part she loved," Bex says.

"What are you talking about?" I ask.

"Laura. You know how the past few years she and I took a trip together to New York City every summer? Whenever we drove past this one part that's all scary-looking, she would squeal, '*Pretty!*' See that over there?" Bex points to the view of skyscrapers looming over the horizon. "That's the part I love about the drive up here. The moment when Manhattan beckons in the distance. When you know something amazing is going to happen. There."

Bex has been beckoned.

It's a good thing I can make myself laugh.

I like my quiet, sleepy D.C. city, but I almost envy Bex her courage in taking on that skyscraper city across the way. Even from this distance, where I can feel that city's pulse and pull, I can imagine that Bex will indeed have amazing experiences at university in NYC. *Please let her not pull Jamal there too.* It's been hard enough imagining losing him to Atlanta, but losing him to New York and to this particular girl—it's too much.

Jason and Jamal are discussing the report from the sports radio station—they're not paying attention to the girls in the backseat. I can speak freely. I turn to Bex. "Do you realize that just this past year alone, your father has voted against immigrant and gay rights bills, made sure the proposed measures didn't even make it out of committee and onto the floor of the House? Do you also know that he repeatedly rejects overtures from D.C.'s token delegate to the House, who, by the way, is not even a real representative—the delegate might as well be a eunuch—to discuss support for a constitutional amendment granting D.C. statehood—"

"*Eunuch?*" Bex bursts into laughter. "You didn't just say that."

I sort of want to be beckoned into sharing her laughter,

but I will not. *Eunuch.* Could I be more of an idiot? I will never make a great orator, obviously. Though with the sensual appeal I hold to the opposite sex, I myself may as well be a eunuch. Maybe I'll just run for D.C. delegate one day instead. Same end result.

"Seriously," I say. "What is with your father's—and his party's—refusal to acknowledge the voting rights of D.C. citizens?"

"What is with your habit of apparently swiping and reading Jim's issues of *Congressional Record* too much?" How did she know I do that! Maybe it was just a good guess. Bex takes a deep breath, then blows her steam. "First, it's completely inappropriate that you—or anyone—would hold me accountable for my father's politics. His opinions and beliefs are his own, and mine are mine. Sometimes I agree with his politics, more often I don't. It's an ongoing debate in my family—but a good one, I like to think. Every step away from the right and toward the center that my father takes, who do you think is pushing him there? *Me.* Second, I often spend parts of my school vacations working in his office, and I happen to know that whatever you may think about his voting record, he's been one of the most active behind-the-scenes members of the House to support D.C. state-hood. He just personally doesn't get along with the D.C. delegate. But he has, in fact, traded support on certain measures with several Maryland representatives in order to line up their recommendations for a retrocession measure to study whether D.C. could become part of

Maryland. Retrocession would allow for a capital city around the Mall for the federal government, but extend Maryland's borders inside the District so that its citizens are granted the same state's rights—and responsibilities—as citizens in any other state. So Dad doesn't just have his own state's constituents he's working for—he's also advocating for those in Maryland and D.C., even if he's not browbeating publicly about it just so he can look like a good guy to the city. Satisfied?"

Absolutely *not* satisfied. "Maryland was originally settled as a refuge for Catholics in Protestant England, and that Catholic influence is still there. Separation of church and state means—"

"Oh, my God."

"What?"

"All this time I wished you would just talk to me, give me the time of day. Now I just wish you would shut up."

A laugh finally lets loose from me.

Quietly, Bex adds, "You sound like Laura. On her better days. The fighter ones."

We return to silence.

The city overwhelms me. So many people, so much noise, so much *rush*—I do not want to be here, not without Laura to share the experience. This was a city Laura loved, with theater and shopping and a landscape she adored, a place where, as she would report when she returned home to me, she could go to feel *alive*.

The boys brought me here on false pretenses—they don't want to be here either. After parking his car in the garage at Jason's grandmother's building, Jason and Jamal immediately hop onto the subway to the Bronx, to go see a Yankees–Red Sox game.

So now not only has Jamal deserted me in favor of Bex, he's deposited me with her as well. Miles is not enjoying being Miles-napped.

"Strand Bookstore?" Bex asks as we stand outside the subway station into which Jason and Jamal have retreated. "Want to go there? It was a favorite of Laura's."

"I never heard her mention the place."

"'Miles and Miles of Books.' Does that sound familiar?"

I can hear Laura's voice now: *I went miles and miles to go to Miles and Miles to bring back books for Miles, my Miles.* She'd sing this to me in the tree house while she handed over a stack of paperback novels in exchange for a nickel bag. She liked to smoke the herb but not to hunt for it herself, whereas I got scolded for hunting inside too many books. It was a good exchange.

"No," I say to Bex. "I don't want to go there. I want to go anywhere that's outside, where I can smoke."

"I know just the place."

Bex plays tour guide, winding us to the Morningside Heights neighborhood and over to the long, wide steps of Low Library at Columbia University, where we sit down behind a statue called "Alma Mater" so I can catch up on my bad habits: smokes and Cokes. From our perch on the steps, we observe the central campus of stately libraries, classroom buildings, and dorms, green lawns with Frisbee and soccer players, families with small children ambling across the central path Bex says is named "College Walk." The campus is magnificent, I have to admit—an academic oasis planted within terra firma Manhattan. A community.

The view elicits the same reaction in Bex and me. It's not something we can control. The tears happen at such random, unexpected times.

We are looking at the future life Laura was supposed to experience, only hers would have been the Georgetown Hoya version.

"Laura and I came to this exact spot last summer," Bex says. "I wanted to show her where I wanted to go to college, take her to the spot where my parents met. And the weird thing is? We're sitting here now, I *know* Laura and I sat here before, and yet I'm not sure the memory is real. Am I missing her so much that I created a happy memory of us here? Was she really with Jason, at a Broadway show, while I came here for the campus visit that day? Or am I really remembering the time we came up here and she was feeling too blue and wouldn't get out of the car, when she asked us to leave her alone so she could nap in the car while Jason and I went sightseeing?"

"I know. Sometimes I'm smoking up in the tree house and I realize I'm talking to her like she's there, recreating conversations we had in the past—only then I ask myself if Laura and I really did have that conversation, or if I only *meant* to with her. Before."

It's news to me that I could share Laura with Bex.

But Bex loved her as much as I did. I could trust Bex on this level.

"Yes. That's exactly it." Bex reaches over for the cigarette in my hand, takes a drag off it, and exhales with no cough (clearly she's experienced), then hands the cigarette back to me. "I'm so relieved you feel that way. I keep wondering if I'm just going crazy."

"Jason," is all I say. Wondering if Bex and I could move up a level. Will she know the question already?

She does. "I think Laura loved him without being in love with him. It's like, maybe Jason offered her a protection from herself. I mean, he's a nice-enough guy, but . . ." She pauses, like she's hesitant whether to say what she really thinks. *Say it, Bex. We both know it.* Amazingly, she does: "There's no *there* there with him. He wasn't a challenge as a boyfriend; being with him was simple. He let in light when she was trying to suppress her own darkness."

"You mean he flanked her?"

"'Flanked'? Where do you get these weird words? But flanked—I guess that's it. Laura could hide behind him." Bex takes my cigarette again, takes another drag, passes it back again. "What about you? Is there any guy you like?"

Emphatically *no*. There's a boy I *love*. She took him.

The question pries too deep. Bex really doesn't understand the tiers.

I shake my head. "What about that stoner Floyd guy?" she asks. "I think he likes you."

I shake my head again. "Good call," Bex says. "That guy's bad news."

Not like Floyd deserves being defended, but still . . . come on! "You didn't think he was bad news that night at Crash Landing when you were getting up close and personal on the dance floor with Jamal while people were spread out everywhere using pretty much every kind of drug you could think of."

"I *did* think Floyd was bad news. I just didn't care that night. It was Jamal's idea to go there. He didn't want you to be alone so much so soon after, but he didn't think you'd agree to go out anywhere else. And I was at a point where I needed something—anything—to help shake off the sadness. So I danced, but I didn't do any drugs. I don't do that. But, listen, okay? That Floyd definitely likes you. Jamal thinks so too. But Floyd is not the type of guy any girl who wants to live past twenty should be going out with. You could do so much better."

Only I can't, and we both know that.

I laugh, the bitter kind. I guess Jamal does love me, in his way. *Shaggy, I've figured it out.* The case of Miles-napping was a setup by Jamal: to give his girlfriend time to talk with me about Laura, and to have a girl set me straight about a bad boy. No way does Bex care whether

I continue to hang out with that Floyd guy. No way there's even a guy out there who'd be interested in me, so what's it matter? Pass me a Scooby snack.

"Can I ask you something?" Bex says. This time she takes my cigarette and finishes it off.

"I think you're going to ask whether I say it's okay or not, so why not go for it." *Like you just did, leveling off my cigarette.*

Bex looks at me, hopeful in her perky brunette way. "Is it okay? Me and Jamal?"

"Okay how?" It's not okay in any way.

"Okay with you. I know what's going on between him and me is sudden, and strange, but it's intense, and feels real. Only I don't want to come between you and him and . . . you know . . . your *friendship* with him?" That word, "friendship." What is she really saying/asking? I have no idea. Or I do, and I deny.

Bex could not possibly know what I feel for Jamal; anybody who could give someone a name like "8 Mile" would have to be assuming a heavy girl would naturally understand that an 8 Mile's deep feelings for a boy could never be reciprocated. The boy goes to the girl like her.

Our trust will not extend into this realm. "Your relationship with Jamal isn't for me to sanction. He'd be the first to tell you that."

"He has. It's just . . . I don't want there to be bad feeling between us. We care for the same people. And I want you on my side. Because Jamal's family, you know . . . they don't like me."

Really?!?!

"Well, they wouldn't share your dad's politics," I say. I'm sure that's all it is. They welcome everybody.

"It's not that."

Really?!?!

"Then what is it?"

"I mean, they like me. Just not with Jamal. They don't say it outright. But I sense it. There's a coldness. It was okay for me to tutor their daughter, to make friends with their son—but to date him? I'm on the wrong side of the color line."

Finally, it's my turn to be on the receiving end of a little piece of peace. Bex has everything: the privilege, the future, the skinny body, the boy. So if the boy's family chooses not to accept her, I have no problem with that. They accept me.

A Nap with Miles

⟡

THE DREAM IS REAL WHILE YOU'RE IN IT.

All those finger-waggers admonishing about what
not to do—*Don't* do drugs! *Don't* smoke! *Don't* drink!—
completely miss that there's a reason people *do* these
vices. They *feel* good, in the moment. The risks and consequences—addiction, disease, a life spiraling downward
out of control, even death—don't matter when you're
inside the *do*.

Inside my nicey-nice dream, here's what *didn't* happen: Bex and Jamal did not sit opposite me and Jason
through dinner at a restaurant near Columbia University
after the Yankees game, kissing and laughing like they
were their own private universe. After dinner, Jason did
not settle his arm along the wide berth of my shoulder
as we walked like the old pals we're not down Riverside
Park alongside the Hudson River, behind Bex and Jamal,
who were oblivious to me and Jason—touching! for no

reason!—and to the fact that the stares their couple-ness generated from people had as much to do with the cocoa-vanilla clasp of their hands as with how attractive they both are. When we reached the Riverside Drive penthouse apartment of Jason's grandmother, away on Martha's Vineyard for the summer, Bex and Jamal did not immediately retreat into the guest bedroom for privacy.

Grandparents really ought not to leave empty apartments to young adults. The naughty games kids play.

I may have been Miles-napped, but I did not travel unprepared. I've abstained since that night at Crash Landing, so the next high could be extra good. This is why *do*ers need to take time off. So the coming back can be even better—a victory lap. Earned.

What I *do* when Jason and I stand alone together in the living room, abandoned, is share with him, from Laura's stash. We sort through the baggie like it's Halloween candy, and settle on two hydros each. It's a sleepover, with no accountability to anyone but ourselves in the morning. We can get as wasted as we want.

We nap but don't nap. We are content. The time-out is about the velvet-smooth feeling, not about the ghost who binds and brought us all here together tonight, she whose absence has so quickly made us so much older, and harder, and sadder.

Because we quickly transport to the dream, the best, best kind, double-dosed, I have no hesitation about doubling up next to Jason on the living room rug. I am not the pudgy, unattractive, unpopular high school girl sharing a secret, intimate moment with the Ivy League, preppy-handsome guy. I am me but not really me. In this moment, I am light, and free, and *perfect*. Wanted.

We're lodged on a floor but floating on a penthouse cloud. Jason and I lie next to one another, on our sides, fully clothed, staring at one another, silently ruminating on our Deep Thoughts without the need to speak. Except when one of us does.

"I never noticed you were so pretty before," Jason murmurs. "Your blue eyes look just like hers." Inside the dream, the real meaning of what he just said is not, *Too bad you don't have her figure, too.*

"Toes," I say. "I like when you feel it in your toes." It's the best part of the high, in my opinion—when the tingle creeps up from your toes, signaling its intent to spread lovingly throughout your body.

Jason reaches for a remote control nestled under a sofa cushion, then presses a button so that his grandmother's classical music starts playing from a stereo. Mozart and hydros: not such a match. So much symphonic furor, it's like führerlike. But any noise that can drown out the beat of headboard-banging, and the sharp, grunting sounds of dreamlovers' ecstasy coming from the other room, is welcome indeed. *Heil.*

Jason's hand moves to touch my cheek.

Outside the dream, I felt sure I would float through my entire life, never touched.

Jason decides to confide. "In our two years together,

we only had sex five times. When she was on medication, she wasn't interested. She said she felt completely
cold. But when she was interested, it was a dare—because
she'd gone off her meds when she wasn't supposed to.
Of course then, I wasn't interested. Not that way. The
price was too high."

Excuse me, I did not ask to be awoken from the
dream.

I could drop the usual clichés to him here:

What happened wasn't your fault.

You will love again.

It's going to be okay.

It's not going to be okay.

He'll never find another love as beautiful as Laura.

He could have taken better care of her, made sure she
took her medication.

Stay inside the dream. Stay inside the dream. No
thought police are allowed to exist there.

I need to comfort him, to keep him inside the dream.
Don't wake up, Jason. Not yet.

I reach over and dare a touch on his nose. It's his
one physical imperfection, broken in a lacrosse match
years earlier. It was the one spot where Laura could
be glimpsed placing an affectionate kiss on her boyfriend. She was not the PDA type. But she loved Jason's
wound.

"Please," he whispers. "Not there."

He takes my hand and places it elsewhere, down
there. His hand guides my hand's touch. And that's all it

is—a light, comforting stroke over his jeans.

I sort of want to float outside the dream so I might remember the moves, in case I have reason to use them on a later victim. Maybe on a boy who'd actually kiss me while leading my hand instead of closing his eyes and just letting it happen to him.

But I respect the dream, and Jason's desire to stay in it.

I think it feels good to make someone else feel good, but I'm not sure.

Since.

We're sitting outside the bathrooms at a rest stop along the New Jersey Turnpike on the drive back home, the next day, me and Jamal, waiting for Jason and Bex to do their business.

We're never alone together anymore.

Sometimes when I am alone in bed at night, in the dark, I drift inside my special dream. There, I am allowed to fantasize that Jamal and I are more than just friends. The special dream doesn't hurt anybody, doesn't cost anything. Who will ever know? There, I have the freedom to cup his face in the palms of my hands, to place tender kisses on his eyelids, to run my index fingers along the arch of his eyebrows, to rub my lips against his. There, he shares my want.

Here, I have to stand by as he stands tall for Bex. He is proud and liberated inside the power of new love.

"Tell me you like her," he says.

"I like her."

"Now say it like you mean it."

The true feelings I have for Jamal have nowhere to go; they might as well drift along the turnpike—aimless, polluted tumbleweed.

"I *like* her." What I mean is, *I accept her. Because I* love *you.*

She's not entirely horrible. She's a lucky girl to have him.

I'm still a little buzzed. It's gonna be okay.

I could be more buzzed. I open my backpack, reach in for the baggie.

"Don't, Miles," Jamal says. "Please don't. For me."

I look up at him. Is he for real? Since when?

I don't. For him.

Jason and Bex emerge from the bathrooms. "Let's go," Jason says. He tosses his keys to Jamal. "I think it's better if you drive."

Jason doesn't look me in the eye, or offer to buy me a Coke for the ride. I understand that what we shared wasn't an experience so much as grief. I could set him at ease and tell him I will respect the rule: *What happens inside the dream stays inside the dream.* But I'm not feeling generous that way, to give him the luxury of that security. Once we return home to D.C., I already know I will never see or hear from him again unless it's by coincidence—and that's fine by me. This case of Miles-napping, this foursome brought together by one dead girl, was a one-off.

But the Bex and Jamal coupling was not a dream.

Wake-up, Miles. Watching them walk hand-in-hand together to Jason's car, so comfortable and pleased to be together, it's clear that the relationship that built in my absence will last even after the grief has passed.

Ask Me

SO MUCH IS HAPPENING AND YET NOTHING AT ALL.

I'm bored.

I'm hungry.

Some things remain the same.

I hate summer. It drags on forever. I'm almost looking forward to going back to school, just for something to do.

Legend has it there are cabals of teenage girls who pass their summers in a flurry of chatterbox-squealing, car-cruising, mall-prowling, and bikini-buying for boy-snaring.

I was never going to be one of those girls. Me, I got a dilettante father in a dilapidated trailer and a rich old guy smoking companion for the summer. Oh, and random, drug-addled boy encounters that don't count in real time.

Nobody's bothered asking me why I've stopped

passing time at the bookstore. The reason is simple. The bookstore literally closed overnight: owner filed for bankruptcy, property sold, padlock on door.

I've lost so much more that's important to me lately, so what's losing a part-time job matter? It's just one more thing.

I read all the books in there already, anyway. I was the store's primary customer.

I've taken on a new mission to fill the hole in my free time, something to hopefully add to my losses: crash diet. Without Jamal to flank me at school, I'll need to present a whole (lot less) new Miles next school year.

Here's how the diet works: Don't eat. Smoke a lot. Cokes are unlimited, as are Junior Mints. Avoid weed-toking as this can lead to hunger pangs.

But, Miles, one might ask, *why not just do speed to drop the pounds? Why do you always have to make things so dif-*ficult?

Thank you for asking, One! The reason is simple. Heart rate-raising forms of artificial stimulation like speed or cocaine scare me. I don't want that much life. I prefer to be numbed out rather than amped up.

If I could just sleep through this summer, I would, but it's challenging when your stash is running as low as your disposable income, and your stomach, running on empty, gnaws at you in extreme hostility.

Jim finds me in the garden at lunchtime. I'm alone in my favorite shaded spot, engaging in my old favorite activities, smoking and reading, as well as my new favorite activity, not eating. Buddy is away on sandwich ministry. Bex and Jamal—I don't even know where they are today. I've stopped asking.

I assume Jim will join me for a smoke, but instead he asks, "Want to come with me to see Miss Lill? I realize it may be hard for you to set aside reading Elie Wiesel's *Night*, but . . ."

"Sure," I say. I set the book down on the bench. I can only do so much Holocaust in a day.

Miss Lill was the longtime housekeeper at Jim's house—she practically raised him. Now she lives in a nursing home. "Lives" may be the wrong word. She *exists* in a nursing home, waiting to die. She's nearly a hundred years old and has mild senile dementia. She's amazing, though—doesn't look a day over eighty.

A trip to a nursing home is just what the doctor ordered (if One had asked). The longer I can stay engaged, the longer I can hold out on food. So far today I've chugged two Cokes and nothing else. Yesterday I held out the whole day until Buddy came home. Then I couldn't help myself. I ate a cheese sandwich. It was good. So good that I was able to chew it for taste, but spit out half the sandwich when he wasn't looking. The black dress that wouldn't zip up the back for Laura's funeral is now loose on me. Pride.

With Laura gone, we're allowed to smoke in Jim's car. She smoked, but only in secret, and only in open air spaces; she didn't like the smell getting into her clothes or hair—for the smell to reveal her. But she's not here now to pass judgment. Once we're in Jim's car and winding through the streets of Georgetown, I place two cigarettes in my mouth and light them with the car's electric lighter. I pass one to Jim.

"Can I ask you something?" I say.

"Ask me."

"How come you never offer to light my cigarettes for me? Like, I can be sitting right next to you while you smoke with a lighter in your hand, but when I take out my own cigarette, you will hand me your lighter, but you never light my cigarette for me. You know, like gentlemen did in those old movies."

Jim chuckles. "I never realized you noticed." He opens the sunroof over our heads to let out the smoke. "As hypocritical as it may seem, I don't light your cigarettes for you because, in many ways, I still think of you as a child. I can't stop you from smoking. I shouldn't even be doing it with you. But extending that light to you seems like it would be an acknowledgment that not only am I condoning our bad habit, but that I'm seeing you as an adult. Which you're not."

"That wasn't an insult, was it?"

"It wasn't." He takes a drag. "I haven't noticed Jamal coming by lately. Everything okay?"

I start to say something that would involve the lie of the word "fine," but instead I say, "He's lost to Bex. It's true love. Supposedly."

Jim's face gives away no reaction other than an exhale of smoke.

I add, "Bex thinks Dr. Turner doesn't like her because she's white. But that's wrong, right?"

His face still gives away nothing, but he doesn't dodge the question. "There might be something to that," he says. "Dr. Turner is from a prestigious D.C. black family whose history in this city goes back to before Civil War times. She graduated Spelman, got her Ph.D. at Howard. And as an educator in the D.C. public system, I'm sure she's seen too many promising young black men lost to incarceration, and the women—mothers, daughters, sisters, girlfriends—that get left behind. I wouldn't be surprised if she'd prefer that the outstanding young black man she raised be reserved for an outstanding young black woman."

"So Dr. Turner isn't a saint, then?" She's as prejudiced as the rest of us. It's almost a relief to know.

"No one's a saint, Miles. And Dr. Turner loves her son. She'll respect any choice he makes, ultimately. But come on now, he and Bex are way too young to be serious. I'm sure this will all pass."

I'm sure it won't.

"How would you have felt about it if Laura had dated someone who wasn't white?"

This is what is happening as time passes—it feels less heavy to speak her name casually.

"The same way I would have felt if she'd chosen to date a woman. Love is love. I'd hope she'd choose a good person, not a race or a gender. I'd hope the same for you."

What if no one ever chooses *me*?

No one ever chose Miss Lill.

She's almost a hundred years old, and in not one of those years did a man step up to marry her, or to make babies with her. When Miss Lill passes, the only family at her grave will be Jim, the old man she raised, who will bury her.

"Botany," Jim would explain to Laura and me when we asked why Miss Lill had no family. She was a loner by nature, more interested in tending nature than in finding a partner. She designed and maintained the lavish gardens at Jim's house when he was growing up; the gardens were the family's gift to her. She would have spent all her time out there if she could, according to Jim. He used to tell us that if Miss Lill had been born a generation later, she'd have followed a path more like Dr. Turner's—maybe she'd have pursued a doctorate in plant science, then gone on to invent plant cures or sculpt the famous botanical gardens in some famous European city—something truly grand and worthy of her brains.

The B-word curse.

Books. I'd probably spend all my time alone and lost in books if I could. It's easier that way. But while I presume this path will lead nowhere in terms of a career, at least I know opportunity exists for me—if I choose to seek it.

Blueberry bellisima. It's the name of the succulent tart made in the bakery down the street from where the bookstore used to be. My hunger is shooting bullets through my body. No boy will ever want me if my body is a balloon.

B-cool, Miles. Maintain. Look up at the blue, blue D.C. sky, don't think about beseeching belly.

Miss Lill lives in a nursing home in northeast D.C. The city is divided into four quadrants: Northwest, Northeast, Southwest, and Southeast. Miss Lill came from Anacostia in Southeast—the slums of D.C., right under the Capitol's nose. Jim would have paid for her to retire and die out anywhere she wanted. She could have stayed in Northwest, where the majority of white people live, on Jim's Georgetown estate and with round-the-clock care, or I bet he'd have paid for her to ride out her last years in the poshest nursing home in the South of France if she'd asked. She didn't ask. But Miss Lill did choose, when she was still able to make that choice, the old folks' home in northeast, home to D.C.'s black working class. By the time she moved there, she'd graduated from regular old assisted living needs. Miss Lill went directly into the Alzheimer's wing of the nursing home.

As Jim and I pass through the corridor, many of this wing's residents sit outside in wheelchairs. Their faces are ancient and fascinating and I want to inspect them more closely, linger, but the mouths on the faces make too much noise, groaning and calling out nonsense words— "STOP!" "Here, kitty!" "ERRRRRRR!" "Go away yesterday!"— that I am too intimidated and freaked to do anything besides keep my head down and be grateful that Jim directs us immediately into Miss Lill's room rather than stop us to say friendly hellos to the Demented Ones.

Miss Lill is sitting up in her bed when we arrive, arranging a vase of flowers in her lap. Her hands shake, so a nurse holds the vase steady for her.

"Jim!" It's a good day. Miss Lill remembers his name. She smiles and passes the vase off to the nurse to take away, then turns to look at me. "Miss Laura, what did you do to your hair? What a *terrible* color." Maybe not such a good day.

Jim steps over to kiss her cheek, and I follow suit. She whispers in my ear, "Laura, honey, no more sweets for you." She pinches a fold of fat on my stomach.

From anyone else, the remark would make me feel hot and shamed, but not from Miss Lill. I wish *I* had senile dementia. There's no accountability—you can tell anyone exactly what you think. It's awesome. Plus, there's less of me to pinch now. I'm a size down from last time we visited Miss Lill. With Laura.

The secret to visiting really, *really* old people is to understand in advance that there's nothing to actually do while you're visiting them. It's not like you can take them out for a movie. It's not like you can discuss what a waste living is. Mostly, you sit around, maybe talk about the weather and the cafeteria food; or, if you're Jim, you can drag out the topic of orchid plants for twenty minutes—I don't know how he stays awake. And when all other topics dry up faster than the dendrobium, you watch TV—very, *very* loud TV. The important part of the visit is already accomplished: showing up.

Laura and I used to like passing the time with Miss Lill by sitting on either side of her bed, massaging her dry hands with lotion, then applying nail polish to her cracked fingernails. This is how I pass the Miss Lill time now, while she watches the Home and Garden channel with Jim and they don't talk about what we're not supposed to talk about with Miss Lill: Laura—the real one, not me, the chubby one.

Hey, Miss Lill, I don't say now, *Did you know Laura and I learned to use off your stash?*

A Laura secret: Miss Lill kept Laura in pills long before we realized there was a dealer we could hit up (Laura was too polite to stoop that low, anyway—but not me, though only for emergency situations). We were fifteen and Jim had coaxed us into a weekend project—to tend to the long overdue task of cleaning out Miss Lill's quarters at his house, where she'd resided for half a century before moving over to the nursing home. Of course Jim had more than adequate resources of other people to take on the project, but I suspect he'd noticed Laura and I spending less time together since starting high school, and he wanted to provide an excuse for she and I to connect. He never made the connection that what we bonded over that weekend was Laura's discovery of a medicine case full of painkillers that had been prescribed for Miss Lill's years of back and neck problems.

If Miss Lill is lucky (and I hope she is), Miss Lill will die peacefully in this nursing home. She'll die in her sleep, the same way Laura chose to go.

I'm pretty sure Laura's passing was peaceful but no one's told me for sure. It's not like I asked to read the autopsy report. My brain works extra hard to block out the fact that one was even filed for Laura.

Jim flips to the History channel when the Home and Garden channel goes to commercial. "Mr. Churchill," Miss Lill announces. "Not a very handsome man." The face on the TV screen is actually Hitler's. I want to tune out, focus on the hand massage at hand, but I can't. Apparently I *can* tolerate more Holocaust today—the television hasn't given me a choice.

In ninth grade, my History class took a field trip to the Holocaust Museum—we didn't have a choice about that, either. (I mean, you could not go. But how much of a jerk would that make you look like?) And the pictures and films at that "museum," the skeletal parade of victims, the gas chambers, the mass burial grounds —it's not like something that could be blocked out. I see Hitler on the TV screen now, but it's the images I've seen of what he caused that blend into my mind's view. And I'm not even high. I don't want to be, either. But I feel it in my veins the way I feel the hunger in my stomach: I *need* to be high. To deal.

When I look, sober, at what humankind is capable of doing, I completely understand the path Laura chose. It almost seems logical.

Miss Lill takes her left hand away and places her right hand in mine, for more lotion. The right side was always Laura's to tend; Miss Lill doesn't want it neglected.

What would Miss Lill's hands have done if they hadn't been held back by prejudices beyond her control? Genocide isn't on par with the evils of racism and sexism, I know that, but I have to consider: Miss Lill's color and gender may have denied her job opportunities, may have relegated her to the back of the bus, but was she one of the lucky ones?

On the one hand, there's a lucky person like, say, Jason, a privileged white kid who's maybe known the sorrow of losing a loved one—but his life will go on, and it's safe to bet he will experience an adulthood that reaps the benefits that come along with being a rich, straight, Caucasian male. On the other hand, there's someone like Miss Lill, who suffered the effects of discrimination and probably knew a lifetime of loneliness hiding out in that garden—but she lies in bed now at the end of her days, doted on by the man she raised, who will spare no expense to make sure her last days are peaceful and that her every need is provided for.

Who suffers more? Neither of them will likely end up as a corpse photo that students casually inspect while walking through a museum that examines the worst of humankind.

How do you measure suffering?

My stomach suffers now from constant, constant craving. Why should I have the luxury of satiating it when so many others can't? Today is camembert in Buddy's product line, but my metabolism will have to settle for caffeine and nicotine. If my twelfth-grade American History class next school year visits any Civil War battlefields (the polite word for "graveyards") in Maryland or Virginia, I hope to be *thin* for the experience.

"Is there freedom from suffering?" I ask Jim. Miss Lill's head has dropped down to her collarbone; maybe the hand massage lulled her to sleep.

"The fact of it or the idea of it?" Jim says.

"The idea of it."

"Freedom." He pauses a moment to reflect on the F-word. "Sometimes I think it's an idea that enslaves us. We're never free from hungering for the notion that we can even have freedom. When perhaps it's the very idea of it that causes us to suffer."

The Epic Battle for the Supremacy of the Cheese Sandwich

It's two lonely ladies up in a tree house, brought to indifferent viewers by a triple-score dosage of Percs, in a milligram count that can deal where simply one or two pills now fail.

In the one corner, we have Miss Miles. She's a superhero, true, but she ain't about nuthin' but the sandwich. She represents for the velvet-smooth (if velvet-smooth means plastic) taste of Velveeta. Her baby blue superhero costume is sprinkled with the initials "CG" across her buxom chest. She's Chubby Girl, the kinder, more tolerant world's new antiheroine heroine. This heroine would never shoot up heroin, by the way. She has *standards*—and knows that needle marks don't make for attractive superhero superskin emblems; her ample flesh shall have to prevail instead. The future of fat people is at stake.

In the other corner, we have Miss Lill. She is the superhero not for a new age, but for the really, really old one. She's "OL"—Old Lady. Her superhero costume is a hospital robe and slippers. She's chronically hunched over, either from osteoporosis or narcolepsy, no one's quite sure. She's a tireless (well, she tries) crusader for the Swiss-cheese sandwich. Once upon a time, she tended the fields that nurtured the cows that produced the milk for the cheese. She *cares* about the quality of the product. When she remembers to care.

Chubby Girl and Old Lady face their showdown at a foldout card table lodged in the middle of the tree house. They shake hands before sitting down at their plates. May the best sandwich win.

A lunch bell rings in the start of the round.

Chubby Girl munches into her Velveeta sandwich within .01 seconds of the bell, but Old Lady doesn't even nibble on her Swiss. There's an epic battle at hand, but she'd rather gab than grab.

"I'm from Switzerland," Old Lady pronounces.

Chubby Girl reeducates her between bites. "No, you're from Anacostia in southeast D.C."

"Same thing," Old Lady says. She touches the soft white Wonder Bread but does not bring its lusciousness to her mouth.

"Um, not really. Ski lodges in the Alps versus D.C. poverty. Two completely different universes." Chubby Girl's sandwich bread is a baguette that's difficult to chew, could be a costly time infraction, but not when her competitor has yet to remember to compete.

"Have you ever been skiing?" Old Lady asks.

"No, skiing scares me. Seems like it requires too much work to reach a high that's too brief."

"I agree. Hey, *there's* my Oxy's! Pass me one, will ya?"

"Surely." Chubby Girl swallows the last bite of her sandwich before Old Lady has even dug into hers. Velveeta has won again. American consumerism always does. And *suh-weet*, there's still dessert to come—crushed and snorted perhaps, to add a little somethin' somethin'?

"More!" the crowd chants. "More!" They want blood. Some people are never satisfied.

"We need to finish the next sandwich round before we can go on to dessert," Chubby Girl whispers to Old Lady. "We've got two rounds to go before the finale." CG eyeballs the next set of plates: Wisconsin cheddar versus Wyoming goat. Who knew Wyoming had it in them?

"WHAT?" Old Lady bellows.

"The crowd craves more. We need to eat more sandwiches."

"No. I already won. Didn't I?" Old Lady looks around at the crowd. *"I gots me some mad botany skillz!"* she raps to them. She then pretends to skat into a microphone: *"Huh-huh huhhuhhuh-huh."*

The crowd roars its approval, throws flowers at O.L., daisies and roses and—someone was really lazy here—weeds.

Chubby Girl doesn't mind the crowd's approval of her competitor, even though she legitimately won the contest. Her belly is full. That's all she really cared about. And there's still dessert to look forward to.

Chubby Girl and Old Lady raise their arms in the air and clasp their hands together, a fantastic freedom fighters' Fernando finale.

Peace prize pills drift down from the sky like confetti.

Time to celebrate.

Sun-slapped

THE SUN IS MY ENEMY.

If I was an evil comic book villain, I would be the one who destroys the sun. I wouldn't destroy it to subvert the world's energy for my own ruthless gain. I'd do it just to do it.

I've read tons of comic books and graphic novels, and from them I've deduced that what makes a great villain is not his or her megalomaniacal plot to ruin the world or to seek revenge on any given superhero. It's the villain's sheer meanness that matters, a driving character force bigger than plot. I admire the single-mindedness.

I single-mindedly crave winter: darkness and cold and big coats that cover up everything. Can't come soon enough for me. I wish it could last year-round.

In my comic book incarnation, after the superhero foils my mission to destroy the sun, I'll probably retire to some Old Folks Villain Home in northernmost Finland, where the sun only appears for an hour a day, and since I am an American who fears other cultures, I won't speak their native language, and we'll just sign with our hands to communicate about basic needs like food and water and my overdue library books. The world will be safe from mean Miles once again.

The long, hot D.C. summer without Laura has extended into extra cruelty: drought. No rain this summer has meant even hotter temperatures, chronic humidity that's turned my hair into a virtual jungle, and a sun that won't go away. The cruelest part is waking up to that sun. I feel it on my face before my eyes open. Hovering in the state between dreaming and waking, the sun's warm glow on my cheeks slaps my consciousness into fake hopefulness: *It's summer. What will Laura and I do today?*

Then I open my eyes and remember.

I dread waking up to that light. Each day it reminds me that Laura is gone, and the world I know is immediately plunged into darkness. It's like the day didn't even have a chance. The sun got to me first.

But worse than waking up to the sun's mean taunt— *Laura is dead, never to share the sun with you again*—worse even than waking up to the sun's warmth pushing a vicious post-Perc migraine inside my head into a hellish *need* for darkness, is the horror of opening my eyes to see Buddy sitting by my side.

At first I don't know where I am. The sun's light shines on the wrong side of my face. A blanket is tangled around my legs; I normally sleep without covers in summertime. Then I remember the previous night: happy pills. I must have fallen asleep inside the tree house, wishing for Laura to share the sleepover.

I kick the blanket away. What kind of sadist would place one on me? "You were shivering in your sleep," Buddy says. He sounds concerned, but slips into sarcasm: "Scratching a lot, too. Tough night?"

I reach for the blanket and pull it over my face, so I don't have to look at him. So I can block out the light.

He won't take the hint to GO AWAY. "Your mother called early this morning. She said it was important she talk to you so I went looking for you and found you up here." I see a shadow movement through the blanket, and sense Buddy's hand over my shoulder, maybe wanting to pat me or something. The hand reconsiders, and returns to Buddy's side. Good choice. "I told Mel you'd call her back later today. You're not in any shape to talk with her this morning."

I don't need to call Mel back. I already know the conversation.

"Mel's not coming back, is she?" I ask. I turn over on my side, away from Buddy. I wish he would not look at me. I wish *no one* would look at me. *Ever.*

"Wouldn't you rather hear it from her?"

Strangely, I wouldn't. "You could tell me," I whisper.

"She's not coming back. She's staying in London with Paul."

Just as I figured.

Good. Now I can truly have the carriage house to myself. I'll turn her bedroom into a library. Maybe I'll find out if I could get a pinball machine in there? I've always wanted one. Just need to find someone to play with me.

I turn back over, remove the blanket from my eyes, look directly at Buddy. He should make the recognition. I'm a big girl. I can take it.

"Could I have a sandwich?" I ask him. Feeding the headache with food sometimes cheats it away. If food doesn't work, I'll need to feed it with more Percs. I have some tucked away inside the pillowcase in my bedroom for just such an emergency.

"Right there waiting for you." Buddy points to the sandwich sitting on a plate on the floor next to me, with a glass of milk alongside it.

"Could you make it a grilled cheese?" I ask. "And a Coke? Over ice?" *And I'm not going to get used to your sandwiches because I know you'll be gone soon enough too.*

He looks puzzled. No one ever asks him to improve on his sandwiches.

"Please?" I add.

Buddy shrugs. "Sure. Sure. Why not."

He'll have to go to his trailer to grill the sandwich. While he's there, I can sneak off to my bedroom and open the pillowcase. Why not just employ both migraine-killing methods simultaneously? I'll be back up in the tree house before Buddy's even flipped the sandwich on his grill. "Tomato on the grilled cheese would be good too, Buddy."

"Great!"

As if my head weren't in enough pain, my eyes take in the painful expression on Buddy's face; the look is painful to *me*, to see him so clearly pleased to be asked.

It's *way* too late to start on tender father-daughter hangover moments.

Buddy starts to walk away, then stops cold at the door. Something's added up in his addled brain. He doesn't turn around to face me, but instead he addresses the door directly with words meant for me. "Miles, I've been there, done that. So if you think you're going to slip off for a boost while I'm out, just know that when I went looking for you this morning, I found your stash. I flushed it down the toilet. It's gone."

Headache and sun be damned, I am out of bed, on my feet, throwing the blanket at him. "HOW DARE YOU!"

Darkness has plunged into apocalypse. I won't make it without. I won't. I can't believe this.

Panic panic panic.

No.

No time for panic. *Think, Miles. Think.*

I shove Buddy aside at the door. I'm the one who's leaving. Not him.

IhatehimIhatehimIhatehimIhatehimIhatehimIhatehim.

"Where are you going?" he demands.

"I'm going to find Jim." Jim will find a way to save me, to make this right. He'll kick Buddy to the curb if I ask him to—at least kick him off the curb of his Georgetown property, to somewhere far away. I know he will. Buddy should be banished to . . . *Virginia.* He deserves it.

This is not happening.

"Good idea," Buddy says. "I'll come along with you. I'll tell Jim why the toilet in the carriage house is clogged and let him know what kind of supplies I'll need to get it cleared out. Unless you think Jim should call a professional plumber instead."

I stop in my tracks.

I'm not going to find Jim. I'm not going anywhere.

I have nowhere else to go.

I Own the Dream

IT'S BECAUSE THE DREAM IS SO PERFECT THAT I CAN WALK
away from it.

Perfection is impossible to attain. It's even harder to
maintain. I can't let myself get so invested in the fantasy.
I should never care that much about *anything*.

I don't want to be a slave to the dream. I need to own
it, and not it me.

Buddy and I have worked out a compromise. He
doesn't tell Jim about my dreamscaping, and I promise
Buddy I'll stop using. Plus, I have to help him in the
mornings to make sandwiches for selling in the afternoon, in lieu of attending a meeting with Buddy in the
evening.

My real punishment is not my new life of sandwiches. It's that no matter the amount of hateful glances
I send his way, or the silent treatment I give him when

I'm sitting at his side wrapping sandwiches in wax paper, Buddy just. will. not. leave.

It's gonna be O!k!a!y!

Buddy must delude himself that he's some kind of healer. Dad of the Year. What he doesn't know is, he only found and flushed Laura's leftover supply that was taped under my bed. He didn't find the super secret stash(es) inside my pillowcase, or the decoy prescription bottles that say Zyrtec or Claritin on the labels but really contain Vicodin and Percoset. Mel never notices when I replace aspirin pills inside her prescription bottles, and keep the good stuff for myself. Miles Score #1: the feel-better pills Mel was prescribed and then barely used after her bunion surgery last spring. Miles Score #2: a double-header, from the painkillers Mel got when her back flipped out, but her digestive system didn't tolerate the relief medication so the doctor gave her another pre-scription instead, and not only did Mel forget about the first prescription left over in the medicine cabinet, she opted to see a chiropractor rather than use the second prescription. Miles Score #3: a Percoset prescription left behind by Mel's London man, Paul, on one of his short-term stays at our place in D.C. I don't care or even want to know why he was prescribed the medication—home run for me!

So the evil mastermind Miles triumphs once again, her super-super stash sitting in Buddy's plain view right inside the bathroom cabinet, and legally prescribed, too—just not to me. I knew my mother would come through for me at some point in my life. Hand me back that trophy, Pops.

Still, supplies are low, the enemy is parked at the curb, and I have no paying job to fund reinforcement stock. I must be careful. Must not get overconfident.

Instead, I eat. I need to be realistic. Without Laura here, food is the only thing I love that loves me back. Why should I starve myself? I'll diet later, after summer, when the heat and sadness and loneliness will likely feel less harsh inside a busy school schedule. Or, I could stop deluding myself that I will ever be thin and desirable and perfect and just get over that fantasy already. Enjoy the food without the guilt—like I do the Percs; inside them, I *am* thin and desirable and perfect.

Buddy's done me a favor, really. Although the withdrawal this time has been harder—take your basic depression that sucks away my energy with or without a fix, now jack it up and add in backaches, headaches, and stomach cramps, and itch itch itchiness—I get by knowing that my suffering will be rewarded. Next time I choose to slip back inside the dream, the fix will be that much more beautiful, brighter, and healing.

I control *it*.

To be on the safe side, I did make a side trip to see Floyd at Crash Landing, to see what backup options might be available. Information is power—and control. When I got there, Floyd explained the going rate for what I crave that Buddy flushed. I don't know if it's the cost of oil jacking everything else up, but whoa, inflation. "Tough times, man," Floyd said, nodding sympathetically. Refueling to quell the fix would hit my wallet harder than the headaches from going fixless. Couldn't there be some hybrid alternative? "We could come to an arrangement," Floyd said, inspecting my chest and my curves. The lechery of his look was not subtle. I left. I am *not* going to be that person. I might crave a quality fix—and a boyfriend prospect—but not that way. The choice was that easy.

I *can* walk away. I've proved it. I don't have a problem with using. It's no more than a guilty pleasure—like smoking and eating. So I'll let Buddy think he won this battle even though it's me who triumphs. This is the choice I make to protect Jim—and the home he has provided for me.

It's possible I'm just being paranoid. I mean, Jim smokes with me on a regular basis. We're partners-in-vice. If he found out about the pharms, he probably wouldn't be pleased. But it wouldn't be a big deal. *Probably*: the operative word upholding the unknown element. The known variable is that I'm not his kid—so why should he care if he knew? It's like Dr. Turner says. I have a dream. Jim would be the last person to deny me it, I bet. However, I would also bet he never knew about Laura's extracurricular pill-popping, and that part I *definitely* wouldn't want him to find out. He's known enough pain this summer.

Thunder and lightning—these were Laura's pain.

But: Rain, at last!

A white light blinding the black night, and the sounds of pounding rain and crackling sky terror wake me at three in the morning, after I've only just fallen asleep (unaided); the constipation and backache that accompany withdrawal make laying still in bed nearly impossible. I hear the violent noise outside the window, and before I've had time for a waking thought, I'm out of bed, running out of the carriage house, to the big house, and up to Laura's room. Basic instinct.

But the princess in the big bed is not in her room, awaiting my comfort.

Jim is there instead, sitting in the chair by her bed, his hands in his face, sobbing.

She's not here waiting for Papa's comfort, either.

I am not sad.

I am furious.

The pain on Jim's face is not a dream. There is no pill strong enough that could kill it, that's how big it is.

She thought that suicide was an escape from her pain. Maybe it was; I don't know. But even counting the painkillers she left me that Buddy flushed, Laura also left behind, for those who had to go on without her, a deeper pain than she could have possibly experienced herself. I will never, ever forgive her for that. I wish I'd never loved her.

This hate burning my heart feels worse than the withdrawal pains thundering through the rest of my body.

"How could she have done this to us?" It's Jim who asks the question. He doesn't wait for my answer, which is good—I don't have one, and I doubt I'm functional enough to articulate right now. His words come in a surge as fast and furious as the rain coming down outside the window. "I should have known. I should have *known*. She was too 'up' right before. Do you remember all the exercising she was doing just before? All the obsessive organizing? The friends—new and old—she was suddenly needing to see? I thought it was just about graduation, that she was excited about starting Georgetown in the fall. I was relieved to see her looking forward to something. How could I have been so blind?"

For once, I am relieved to be outside the dream. The Laura I loved before—not the one I hate now—would want me to be fully present for her father in this moment. I feel it. Her.

I'd be the last person who could impart wisdom on Laura's motivations to Jim. That is, I couldn't offer him any insight into her last days that would give him comfort rather than more pain.

So I don't say anything. I go sit by the side of the bed next to him, and just listen.

This, I can do.

First Lady: Not a Job
I'd Want

❦

I AM LARGE AND IN CHARGE. I'VE GONE FIFTEEN DAYS without a boost. This is a first for me since I was fifteen.

We've marked our summer in firsts: first Independence Day weekend without Laura throwing a garden picnic for us; first fireworks heard from the Mall without Laura cowering under her bedcovers in fright from the noise, even though she heard the explosions every year and knew what to expect; and now, our first—and only, this year—Georgetown summer garden party/political fundraiser without Laura wearing that year's prettiest blue cocktail dress and acting as Jim's hostess (unless she had a black-mark day, in which case she could be found, as on red-white-and-blue day, underneath her covers).

This first garden party without Laura is a political fundraiser hostessed by Dr. Turner—with an able helping hand from her First Lady, Niecy, who is wearing a beautiful princess dress and an eager debutante smile. The object of celebration is Dr. Turner's sister, who is planning a run for D.C. city council. The people the family is here to meet and greet, by way of a guest list culled by Jim and Dr. Turner, are the assorted members of the D.C. gay hierarchy—business leaders, lobbyists, lawyers and socialites who wave their rainbow flags high, and use their financial clout to support their political agendas. Gaining favor with these constituents' dollars and their dogmas is crucial to any serious contender for local political office. The federal part of our city may be overrun by Congressional conservatives who criticize the lifestyle, but the District's residential population is substantially populated, particularly in Northwest, by those inside "the life."

I used to hide out in the tree house during these parties, observing the party people without having to participate, while Laura put on her best "show" face and presided with her proud papa. I was never missed.

This year I participate. At least, I show up. Someone's got to smoke in a remote corner with Jim through this first without Laura, to stand by his lonesome side. The benefit of this benefit is that Buddy left for the weekend. Since his trailer could potentially scare away party goers and their checkbooks, Jim very politely asked Buddy to make a temporary exit. I'd like to very not politely ask Buddy to make it a permanent one, but I can't until I can be sure he won't out my not-problem to Jim.

"Would you care for a drink, Lady Miles?" Jim asks me.

"I don't care about anything," I remind him.

He returns to our remote spot with a Coke for me. I hand him a lit cigarette.

We're standing in the corner of the garden, away from the central party gathering area. Our usual sacred smoking space is now covered with a canopy, under which professional waitstaff serve drinks and hors d'oeuvres to guests. The smokers—and Jim and I are the only ones— stand at a respectful distance at the garden's rim, observing, as our smoke drifts up and away into the hedges.

I'm already thinking what Jim speaks aloud. "Feels strange to see people assembled here again. I've lived at this house my whole life, hosted parties here probably hundreds of times over the years, yet this one feels like it may as well be attended by aliens for all that I feel I belong here right now."

"I think we're the aliens, not them," I say. They are so vibrant in their champagne chatter. We are still dragging lead weights around our ankles. Will they ever unshackle?

I wear my basic black balloon dress, and would never dream of fitting into their couture. "I'm a disappointment as a teenager," I tell Jim.

He shakes his head, smiling. "How do you figure, Miles?"

"Niecy over there, she is a good teenager. She's got

the right clothes, the right looks. Notice she's meeting and greeting with her mom and her aunt, but also scoping out the young people here with their parents. She'll have five movie dates for next week before the night is done, I guarantee it."

"That's not indicative of being a teenager. That's called being an extrovert." He points to an attractive couple, two young men, standing in the distance, at the fountain, holding hands. "I've never gotten used to that—I think that qualifies *me* as the disappointment. All the years I've fought for them to have the right—no, the *comfort*—to do that, and still, when I see it, I'm never not surprised. Here's a laugh for you, Miles. When I was their age, so very much wanting to be empowered and emboldened in my identity, I actually tried to be flamboyant, tried to be a queen. I could never pull it off. At heart, I was and am just a boring old white man with an accountant who likes his plain white shirts to be French-pressed."

The image of Jim as a young queen *is* funny. "Did you ever wear a rhinestone tiara?"

"I did."

"Then you weren't a disappointment."

"Oh, but I was. It was a genuine Tiffany tiara that had belonged to my mother."

"That's just sick. Not disappointing."

Jim raises his glass to me. "Cheers, Miles."

I clink my glass of Coke to his champagne. "Cheers, Jim—Queen of Stodgy Ol' Georgetown."

"Ol' J. Edgar would have envied me, back in my time."

"I'm so sure."

The shackles loosen.

The moonlight, the garden, the champagne—these elements must be inspiring if you're young and in love. The two men at the fountain share a tender kiss, lost to each other—and to the two smokers peeping on their romantic moment.

"Do you think they take for granted the rights you and your generation fought for?" I ask Jim. I will never share a romantic moment like that with someone. The best I'll ever get is inside the dream. Or watching it from a smoking distance.

"If we did our job right, they do," he answers.

IwantmydreamIwantmydream.

"Can I bum a smoke?" The question is posed by one of my people: a teenage freak. Green mohawked hair, a nose ring. He's wearing sloppy punk gear—tight black jeans, combat boots, a worn-out and holed T-shirt. I recognize him as the son of the two women I can see engaged in conversation with Dr. Turner's sister over by the drink station.

"No," Jim and I both say at the same time.

Disaffected, angry young punk boy gives good pout. He folds his arms over his chest and grumbles, "I don't see why I had to come to this stupid party anyway. What do I care who runs for D.C. city council?"

Jim asks him, "Do you care that you have to register for the draft when you're eighteen?"

"Guess so," Punk Boy grumbles.

I rally to Jim's cause. I almost know the speech by heart. I say, "As a D.C. citizen, you will have to register for the draft, and enlist in the military if called—but your own elected representative will have had no influence in the decision to go to war. Yet, you serve. Possibly die, for their war. So the hope is that electing the right representatives to D.C. city government can be a step toward gaining influence with Congress, to lobby for D.C. statehood. To give you as a tax-paying D.C. citizen who serves his country the same voting rights and influences as the citizens of the other fifty American states."

Jim leans in to me. "You're doing an excellent job of not caring about anything, Miles."

Now it's Bex who's found us. "Hi!" She grabs my arm. "Can I borrow her, Jim?"

She doesn't wait for his response but leads me away toward the house, where Dr. Turner and Jamal are standing in the open doorway at the main entrance. Dr. Turner is not bothering with her usual polite tone of voice. She's hot in conversation with her son. "Now is not the time for this, Jamal . . . *Atlanta* . . . you're going to *Atlanta* next week if it's the last thing I do . . . I am not hearing this, Jamal."

"Don't tell me," I say to Bex. "You want me to flank you."

"Please?" she asks.

Moonwalking

PEBBLES AGAINST MY BEDROOM WINDOW. THREE A.M. Just like old times.

It will be easier when he's gone.

No more than a few hours have passed since Jamal's blowout fight with his mother that ended with her storming away from the party she was throwing at Jim's house, then Jamal taking a tearful Bex home. A full moon hangs in the night sky as I open my bedroom window to see Jamal standing outside, waiting to perform his grand finale.

Jamal moonwalks for my moonlit viewing pleasure. The crickets sing their approval.

He smiles up at me from down on the ground. "It means a lot to me that you stood up for Bex when it counted," Jamal says.

I didn't, really. I just stood by her side, held onto Bex's arm, as Dr. Turner had a full-on public meltdown that her son had chosen that girl, and this particular bad time, to stake his claim.

"'The desired effect is what you get when you improve your interplanetary funksmanship,'" I tell him from my side of the window.

"'Chocolate-coated freakin' habit-forming,'" he answers.

I grab a pack of smokes from my nightstand, slip my feet into my Chucks, and go outside to find him.

"Let's take a walk," he says. "I'm gonna be gone for good soon. I hardly saw you at all this summer. Let me see you now."

"I'm wearing my pajamas."

"So what!" He points to my Cookie Monster pj top and does his best impression of the furry blue beast. "Me want *cookie*! And a walk with Miles!"

Jamal grabs my hand and pulls me toward the gates of Jim's property. He's skipping in glee.

As a heavy smoker, not only do I not run, I don't skip. Cough cough. Instead, I loosen my hand from Jamal's, set him free—no touch, no touch, bad bad bad—but I do follow his wandering. I'll walk anywhere, across the uneven, cobblestoned streets of Georgetown in the middle of the night, in pajamas, even, for him. Especially since I am sober and can truly appreciate the historic house scenery under the yellow moon, the balmy D.C. night, and can have Jamal all to myself for once.

"You are way too happy for a boy who just broke his mama's heart," I tell him. "And whatever could have compelled you to choose a party your mom was throwing to make your announcement to her?"

"I have no idea!" Still ahead of me, Jamal turns around and moonwalks again so I can see his beautiful face announcing his bliss. "When the spirit moves you, ya gotta go for it, I guess. But after I dropped Bex off at home, I called Mama from the car to apologize. She was calmed down. We had a good talk. She's got a sorority sister from college who lives in Harlem, owns a brownstone there. Mama's going to call her friend and see about me staying with her while I get settled in New York, find my way. We made a compromise. She supports me going to New York, I agree to take part-time community college classes there, once I'm settled."

"So you're not planning to move in with Bex, then?"

"No way! It's *love*, man—but we're way too young for that. Bex has got college to start. I've got the struggling actor life to figure out. We just want to be close, keep this thing we've got going, going. College life, right now, that wasn't what I wanted. And I felt that way before I got together with Bex. Her moving to Manhattan to go to Columbia just gave me inspiration to make the choice I wanted to make anyway."

"And Bex?"

"What about her?" The moonwalk stops. He's looking directly at me. The unspoken words are our own little dance.

Does he know? What I can never say to him?

"Your family. Do they accept Bex?"

"They're adapting. This wasn't expected."

"What about her family?" What about how Jamal got a girlfriend, fell head over heels in love, and completely changed the course of his life this past summer, while I just smoked and grieved and watched it happen from a pharmed-out distance.

Jamal laughs. "Oh, *her* family is a lost cause entirely! They're never going to like their baby girl making this choice. A *Negro*! Imagine! Politically, however, it would look bad not to put a bright spin on it, so . . ." Jamal moonwalks again, but with a pained, stiff expression on his face as he performs an impression of Congressman Same Old White Man. "'Jamal, young man. Welcome. Do you come to us with any NAACP leadership members in your family whom we might invite to Thanksgiving?'"

"Will you miss me?" I ask Jamal.

It's the best I can do.

"'Course I'll miss you. Not like I've seen that much of you this summer."

"That was your choice," I say. "You chose Bex."

"No. I came by for you plenty. You don't even realize how often I came by just to find you passed out with a book on your lap. I think *you* chose solitude. *You* chose pills."

This is some kind of hypocrisy that I will not tolerate.

"*You've* used before. So why do I feel like you're criticizing *me* for it?"

"*I* have experimented. Enjoyed it in those few moments, but don't feel the need to experiment further. Had my fun. Moving on."

I can't fake it anymore—being around him and acting like my heart doesn't matter.

I'm glad he's moving on. Go, already.

Bex has done me a favor. Once they've taken off for their enchanted Manhattan universe, the hurt can't hug itself around my heart, squeeze me to death. Not if they're not here in D.C. to remind me of their hap-hap-happiness. Yay for Us, Couple of the Century!

Flick.

Out of sight is out of mind.

Being in control of the dream means knowing that a responsible user does not use to escape stress.

I am not stressed. I'm free. Free at last! I can go out of mind.

I'm over two weeks clean. Buddy is away for the weekend. I've got my secret stash. I've *earned* the fix.

I think Jamal's still talking—*Please get help, Miles, blahblahblah*—but say what? I've got a plan.

I've hardly eaten anything for the last eight hours, almost like I knew without knowing that tonight would be the night for the grand return. On an empty stomach, the treat will last longer, tingle sweeter. *Yes!* Nownownow.

Buh-bye, Jamal, I'm going back home, back to bed. Have fun in New York, hope you have the time of your life—like I plan to once you're gone!

The Category 5 hurricane has made landfall. Time to batten down the hatches and ride out the perfect storm.

The Game

THE GAME I PLAY IS THIS:

Close window blinds.

Crank up A/C.

Harness happy hydros in hand.

Insert on tongue.

Chug-a-lugga H_2O. Wash away yo' cares!

Perform private happy dance standing on the bath-room floor.

Go to room and jump onto bed.

Wrap large-and-in-charge body inside covers.

Wait.

Sing song to self:

Lying in bed/wishing I was dead.

Refrain.

Lying in bed/wishing I was dead.

Jump-starting the dream before the tingle truly sets in is totally allowed.

It's a garden wedding, summertime, eighty degrees and no humidity! Bex and Jamal stand before the minister under a trellis covered in honeysuckle, Niecy by their side as their maid of honor. The bride says her vows. The groom starts to declare his, then . . . he turns to Bridesmaid #8. "Miles, you're the one! Only you! Can you ever forgive me for not realizing it sooner? My darling, Miles—hollaaaaaaaaaa for me, baby!" The bride, too, turns to Bridesmaid #8. "He's right, 8 Mile. Can you ever forgive me for living out this lie when all along, this was supposed to be your dream?" The maid of honor adds, "Miles, I'll braid your hair in the carriage house right now and we can come back out and have us a proper wedding! You and my brother. We! Are! Family!"

No, no, no. That fantasy's tired, needs to be *re*tired. The dream *does* cost something; the dreamer eventually wakes up.

New dream.

Reset.

It's a tree house party, hot hot hot summertime steaming up through the wilted honeysuckle outside, two baked sister-cousins inside. Sadness has swallowed them. They've made a pact to escape the sadness, together. Swallow it all away. "Do you think . . . after . . . will we be able to see the ones we've left behind?" the heavy girl asks the light girl. "No," the light-of-body-but-heavy-of-mind girl answers. "We won't be able to see their suffering. We'll have evaporated. Just

like that. What they feel won't matter if we're nothing."
The heavy girl can't believe the light girl could so casually
dismiss those who will be left behind. Surely there should
be more debate. But the light girl is ready. It's now or
never. The light girl raises her pretty hand to toast their
end, but the heavy-of-body-but-maybe-lighter-of-mind
girl hesitates: "I'm not so sure." Because really—if the
dead cannot witness the mourning of the survivors who
have fought for and sometimes hurt but always loved the
departed, what's the point of making such a grand statement? This is a mistake. *Words.* They need to share words,
not pills. The hesitating girl throws a piece of rope down
to the garden from the top of the tree house—a lifeline.
She needs to get them out of here. OUT! Now! *Please!*
Panicpanicpanic. She can't stop this. It's too late.

This is a weird game this round. Someone's not playing fair.

What happened to the dream? Only emptiness.

Where is the tingle? Where is the floaty?

Go back to square one.

Read over game rules carefully. Just as suspected—
the rules state nothing about cold/clammy/nausea/
slooooooowwwwww breathing. Point violation!

Clearly it's time to call in a referee. This game is not
going right.

But requesting the lifeline is challenging when the
numbness makes movement feel impossible. Bummer.

The rules should be rewritten.

Visitors

THE DREAM IS DEAD.

I am not.

Bex saved my life.

Now we're stuck with each other forever. I think that's how it works.

Before I resign myself to this fate, I'll need some answers from her.

"Why did you name me '8 Mile'?" I say to her. She's sitting in the visitor chair by my hospital bed, flipping through a magazine.

She glances up from the pages. "You're awake. I didn't realize. What did you say?"

"I said, 'Why did you name me '8 Mile'?"

The expression on her face veers from tired to incredulous. "You wake up in a hospital bed after an overdose, and that's your first thought?"

"Yes."

Actually, my first thought upon stumbling into consciousness, as I felt the plastic hospital band around my wrist and looked around the sterile room, was, *This is nothing like in books or movies.* In fantasy world, the heroine wakes up, surrounded by loved ones, and precociously asks, "What happened? I don't remember anything." Usually she has a pretty ribbon in her hair and roses by her bed.

My hair is a tangled jungle, it smells like puke, and no one's sent me flowers.

There is not one single moment I don't remember. I remember my greed with the pill count; it was about gluttony, not about making a statement. I remember gluttony's reward: panic and nausea, coupled with the complete inability to act on either. I remember the sweat pouring from my skin despite the freeze shivering my insides. I remember my heart not wanting to beat. I remember not being able to stand up to answer the doorbell. I remember feeling surprise to see Bex standing over me, dialing 911; I remember feeling even deeper surprise that I hadn't remembered it was she whom I'd managed to call to say only, "Please help me."

I should write that part down. Over time, I may forget that part. Or revise it to change the key players.

"WHAT DID YOU TAKE? WHAT DID YOU TAKE?" I remember trying to tell them, but they didn't believe me. I will never, ever forget the terror as the medics stuck the tube inside my nose and ran it down to my stomach. I will never, ever forget the gagging from the tube, like a tongue depressor at the back of the throat, only a million times worse. I will always remember trying to push the doctors away, cursing them as torture monsters, while silently thanking them for doing the job for me—allowing me to live. I will always remember the black from the charcoal they used to pump my stomach. The charcoal got all over my face, their hands, my clothes, their clothes. That blackness brought me out of the nightmare and into this morning's light.

I lived, but the black lingers. It's still smudged on my hands, my hospital gown, the hospital blanket. It's probably on my face, too—at least it's still visible on Bex's face.

"You are honestly the most confusing person I've ever met," Bex says.

"I'm flattered," I say. "But I really did not appreciate that name."

She slams the magazine closed. "I called you '8 Mile' 'cuz I thought you were clever with words, like that rapper. It was supposed to be, like, a play on words."

"The play on words could also be taken to mean 'fat girl.'"

"Well, it wasn't intended that way. Why do you always assume the worst in people?" Her face, tinted with charcoal marks on her left cheekbone and right eyebrow, looks at me even more incredulously. "You don't actually expect me to apologize?"

"It'd be nice," I say.

She looks like she wants to hit me. Then: "I'm sorry. Satisfied?"

Satisfied. "I'm sorry too," I say. And: "Thank you."

This part's cool. The dialogue is just like a movie.

Shrink: "Are you trying to kill yourself?"

Me: "No. I think this is a pretty sucky world we live in, and I don't necessarily think there's that much worth living for. But I don't want to die, either." I didn't necessarily believe these words until I just heard myself say them. *I don't want to die.*

The attending psychiatrist is here to determine my immediate fate—whether I will be released from the hospital, or admitted to the psych ward instead. Her questions, our dialogue, is meant to diagnose my level of "suicidal ideation." I've read about it in books. Only now I'm the girl cast in the fairy tale, an 8 Mile princess with black marks and the smell of human waste tainting her skin.

Shrink: "Do you have access to a gun or other firearms?"

Me: "No." *But when D.C. becomes a state and I become sheriff, I'm running the NRA out of town.*

Shrink: "Do you have a plan to kill yourself?"

Me: "No. I couldn't go through this again. The only plan I have is to not find myself back here again."

Shrink: "That's a good plan." She jots some notes on my chart, then stands up to leave. "I'll be back later today to talk with you and your family about long-term treatment after I sign your release forms. You can go home this afternoon. But your work is only beginning. That is, if you truly don't want to come back here like this. Any questions for now?"

So, so many questions.

But there's only one I want answered by her. To directly ask those who care, who already know the answer, would be too hurtful to them. "Do you know how she died?"

When the shrink came in, she let me know she'd already consulted with Laura's psychiatrist, and that she was aware of "the situation" of the other girl who was brought to this same hospital a few months back, only dead.

"Do you really want to know?"

I *do* know. Laura swallowed some happy pills and slipped inside a long, dreamy sleep, like a good, pretty princess.

But maybe there's more to the story.

I nod.

The shrink says, "Laura died from choking on her own vomit. That's how people who try to commit suicide with pills very commonly die. Not from the Valium, as Laura tried, but from her body trying to reject the ingestion. Commonly in these situations, the stomach contents come up to the back of the throat, but the body is sedated to the point that the vomit slides down into the lungs. It's the choking from that secretion going into the lungs that causes death. The suicidal person thinks they've chosen a peaceful end. In fact, they've chosen a particularly gruesome one. I've seen Laura's autopsy report. Her case was not an exception."

It's like Buddy's excited to see me here. He looks elated rather than burnt out, and doesn't bother affecting a somber tone to his voice. He sounds very *up!*, despite the downer situation. "I've been waiting for you to hit rock bottom, kid. Was hoping you wouldn't take it this far. Glad you lived to tell. Time to make that health insurance pay for itself!"

He hands me a stack of rehab pamphlets for residential treatment clinics in Maryland and Virginia. The top one is seemingly related to his tribe. It says "Narconon." The next brochure promises: "Free yourself from cravings, guilt, depression."

Propaganda. "Are you aware that Narconon is a front for Scientology?" I ask my father.

"No!" he says, surprised. He plucks that pamphlet from my hand and tosses it into the trash. "You're too damned smart for your own damned good. I don't know what I'm supposed to do with you."

"I feel the same about you."

We laugh the same laugh. It might be the one trait we share, besides addiction.

"I'm not going anywhere," he says. "So just get used to me already."

"What about Mel?"

"She's been called. She's trying to make a trip home. . . ."

"I want *you* to stay."

I'm not just using him for his sandwiches. Buddy chose to be here when it counted; he *wants* to be here. My mother does not.

There's probably only one person in the universe whom I would allow to smother my face in kisses, and that person is my high school principal.

Kiss on my right cheek. "Oh, my God, Miles." Double peck on my left cheek. "How could you?" Smooch smooch smooch on my forehead. "Thank you, Jesus. Thank you for allowing her to live." Her grande finale is a gentle slap to my chin. "If you *ever* get into trouble like this again and don't come to me for help, I will personally take you out of this world myself."

I hold up my arm for Dr. Turner to inspect my wristband, inscribed with my name as a patient at Georgetown University Hospital. "Looks like I'm college material after all," I say.

She doesn't laugh. "Guess what, wisemouth? You've also been elected the editor of the school newspaper. Congratulations. Between your recovery program, schoolwork and the newspaper, you're going to be one busy lady this fall. Not so much time alone, hiding things—that's *my* plan for you."

"Our school doesn't have a newspaper."

"It does now. I'm thinking the first issue will be dedicated to educating the student population about D.C. statehood issues and volunteerism to that cause. Good luck."

She's serious, but she's also fronting. She doesn't want me to notice the person not here.

"Where's Jamal?" I ask her.

She *still* won't lie to me. "He's pretty mad at you, honey. I couldn't get him to come here today."

Oh.

"Maybe later?"

"Maybe."

She doesn't sound convinced.

Jim.

This one feels worse than the catheter did.

I've already seen him sitting by one girl's bedside, sobbing.

"I can't do this again, Miles," he says, stone-faced, to the other girl.

Do I still have a home?

I need to say just the right thing. I have no idea what that is. What could she have told him to give him comfort?

"Laura didn't want help. I do." I might fail. But I'll try.

"Good." His voice sounds cold. Defeated. "A counselor from a private clinic will be coming by the carriage house tomorrow to talk with you." He, too, hands me a pamphlet. But it's for a local treatment clinic for depression and substance addiction, an outpatient program.

I wouldn't have to go away. I don't want to leave D.C. Or him.

I want him to offer me a cigarette, some words of encouragement, I wouldn't mind some M&Ms, he could throttle my neck, even—I'd take *anything* not to see the blank stare his gray face sends my way.

Silence.

I only wanted to slip inside *my* dream, not Laura's. The OD part was an accident. "I didn't mean to do what Laura did," I say.

I only need one thing in order to leave the hospital. It's not a home, or a counselor, or a program.

Longer silence.

"I believe you," Jim finally says.

That's what I needed.

A Ritual Last Smoke

ONCE UPON A TIME, A FRESH-FACED YOUNG GIRL, WHO'D just cheated death by having her stomach flooded with charcoal to pump out self-administered, illegally-obtained toxins, celebrated her eighteenth birthday at a small party thrown in the lavish garden on a beautiful-sad Georgetown estate.

In what she hoped would be her last act of chemical dependence (besides quitting nicotine and sugar—she figured those would be Steps 13 and 14, and she'd worry about 1-12 for now), the birthday girl had transformed her appearance. No, she had not miraculously dropped fifty pounds, or sacrificed her black wardrobe, or even let loose the lip ring that cut through her few attempts at smiling. She'd simply gone back to her roots.

"You look better as a blonde," said Niecy, her hair colorist. Niecy had also been assigned the supporting role of Secondary Best Friend until Niecy's brother, the boy moving to New York who would not come to the birthday party, forgave the birthday girl. It was a good enough exchange, for now. "Can I flat iron your hair too? Let me make it all smooth to really show off that fairy-light color."

"No," said Miles, the blond bombshell. She scrunched her hands in her wavy hair, to further curlify its fullness. "Big is the new beautiful."

"Jamal sent you something from Giant," Niecy said.

Miles did not have to ask what the boy had sent in place of himself. Her mouth could already taste it. Who else but him would know she wouldn't want a fancy birthday cake from a fancy Georgetown patisserie, but would prefer their shared favorite—the grocery store sheet cake with the psycho plastic clown perched in the middle?

"Those cakes are so disgustingly sweet," Niecy said. "I'm gonna have two pieces."

"Will you tell him something for me?" Miles asked.

"He'll come around, Miles. You know my brother. Can't stay mad at a lady."

"It's okay. You don't need to try to make me feel better about it. It's probably better for us to be apart for a while. He's got his exciting new life to start without me dragging him down, me in my exciting new life of an addiction treatment program and tagging along to AA meetings with my father. But could you please give this message to Jamal? Tell him: I already know the words. I just need to learn the beat. This tone-deaf white girl will try to make music out of recovery."

She meant the message. She didn't know if she would survive it. Her stomach had been purged and her body released—alive—from the hospital, and yet the cravings had the audacity to already set back in. She found it strange to feel so relieved not to have to hide the cravings anymore. To acknowledge them. She wished for Jamal to think her strong enough to make it through. She wished that for herself, as well.

"I will tell him," Niecy said. "That's a good message. Think you could reword it to rhyme? He'd like that. Now get on out of this carriage house. There's a party waiting for you outside. Today is the day to be Miles."

It's not like a difficult girl who could count all her friends on one hand had a large gathering waiting in the garden to get their party on. She had a Niecy, a Dr. Turner, a Bex, a Buddy, a cake from Giant, some cheese sandwiches . . . and an old man smoking on a bench under a tree house.

She knew where to find him.

"We've got to stop meeting like this," she told him. She was very, very tired—but never too tired for him.

He looked up and choked on his exhale. "Your hair!" he said. She could see the recognition in his eyes, but he didn't say it: *You look like our beloved gone girl.*

She sat down on the bench next to him. She'd

neglected to bring her cigarette pack outside; this craving she was in no way ready to sacrifice. But she'd have to wait for him to offer.

What he offered was this: "You and I have an appointment at the DMV tomorrow."

"But I don't want to drive," she said.

"No one's saying you have to. But you need to get a D.C. identification card." She started to protest but he stopped her. "No, I don't need to hear the enslavement of D.C. speech. It goes nowhere. You need to be able to register to vote."

"Why bother? My vote counts for nothing."

He shook his head in frustration. "God, Miles—"

"Do you believe in God?" she interrupted him. That all-powerful, omniscient He seemed a more worthy subject of debate than impotent D.C.

"You'll be surprised to know, but I do."

"Well, according to a disturbing percentage of fundamentalist voters in this country, He doesn't believe in you. So I don't see why I should register to vote when my voting in D.C. means nothing against their legitimatized votes."

"Think about it this way. I doubt I will ever make those fundamentalists accept me or my choices. But I can subvert them at every possible turn at the same time. I can fight back. I can fund a school for queer youth. I can make friends with influential politicians. And I can pursue my agenda at those voters' expense, too. All those vacuum cleaners with my family's name on them that get bought by Bible Belt consumers are funneling money to my causes. There's hope. And if you don't have hope, what do you have?"

He had made hope possible for her.

She said, "I don't believe in God, but if I did, I'd hope He would approve of your subversive methods. And I'll do it. Register to vote. But not because I believe my vote will count. But because you asked me to."

"Thank you. I'll take it." He stubbed out his cigarette into the ashtray she'd reached under the bench to place between them. "Do you believe in anything, my dear?"

"Yes. You."

He laughed. "It's official! You've gone as soft as your original hair color. It's obviously time for me to leave."

This could not be happening. "Not really?" she said, almost hushed. The ground felt so firm next to him. He couldn't swipe that from underneath her. Not now.

"Really," he said. "It's time. I see you registered to vote, you can see me off on a train from Union Station tomorrow. I need a long journey."

"Where are you going?"

"I don't know. Key West? Vancouver? Probably Provincetown is as far as I'll make it. Change of scenery will do this broken heart good."

"You'll be back?"

"Soon."

"How soon?"

"Soon enough."

It was like the world had gone suddenly dark to her, then immediately opened back up—with the hope for his soon-enough return.

She had one last question. It was the most important one. "But who will smoke with me?"

He took two cigarettes and a lighter from his shirt pocket. He handed her one cigarette. "I couldn't say," he said. "This is my last cigarette. I vow it. Of course, I had to share the ritual last smoke with you. It's a tradition with smoking buddies. But after this one, the vice is yours to ruin your health on your own. You know the consequences. I can't be helping you out in this department."

He took a drag on his last cigarette as she placed her not-last cigarette in her mouth. She waited for him to hand over his lighter.

He leaned over to her instead.

He lit.